Anna and Mo Maybach
with puzzles & riddles by Inka and Markus Brand
Translated by Britta Norris

THE DRAGON'S CAVE
A Puzzle Adventure

T0413797

PUZZLE
WRIGHT
JUNIOR

JUNIOR New York

WELCOME!

Do you enjoy reading exciting stories and love puzzles? Ready to follow the clues in a legendary adventure? Then EXIT: The Book is perfect for you. It's packed with secrets and exciting riddles for you to crack! But don't worry if you get something wrong – no need to deep-six the book! To help you, there are clues and answers for each riddle on pages 11–13 of Lucia's Secret Book, which is located at the back of this book. Page 11 also explains how to use the clues correctly. But only use them if you really need them! At the end of the story (page 137), count the number of clues you have left. The fewer clues you need, the better your result will be.

Before you start reading, cut out the three colored strips (red, blue, and yellow) on pages 15 and 16 of Lucia's Secret Book, then insert them through the color-matching slots in the front cover flap of this book (also, read page 14 of Lucia's Secret Book).

Sometimes in the story, at the end of a page, you will be asked to continue reading from another page in the book. Follow these instructions. Soon you will come across a riddle that you must solve to crack a three-digit code. This will give you the page number you need to continue reading.

For some puzzles, you'll need scissors, a pen, or a sheet of paper. You may need to cut, label, crease, or fold things. But only cut out things with a dotted line around them and if instructed to do so!

And one more tip: throughout the book, you will find words written in capital letters. Write them down next to the corresponding symbols on page 7 of Lucia's Secret Book.

Here's a quick recap:

1. Cut out the decoding strips on pages 15 and 16 of the Codex (at the back of the book) and insert them into the color-matching strips in the front cover flap.

2. Start reading Lucia's story on page 005. Continue reading until you are told to go to a different page, or there's a riddle to solve.

3. Solve the riddle. (Get ready to draw, cut, and fold). The solution is always a three-digit code which you must enter using the decoding strips. Turn the strips over to get the page number on which to continue reading.

4. If you get stuck, you can find clues to help you in Lucia's Secret Book (pages 11–13 at the back of the book).

5. Work your way through the whole book, solving each riddle as you go until you get to the end. Now start reading on page 005.

PUZZLE
WRIGHT
JUNIOR

JUNIOR New York

PUZZLEWRIGHT JUNIOR and the distinctive Puzzlewright Junior logo are registered trademarks of Sterling Publishing Co., Inc.

English translation © 2024 Sterling Publishing Co., Inc.
Illustrations and original text © 2019 Franckh-Kosmos Verlags-GmbH & Co. KG, Stuttgart, Germany
Original title: Brand, Maybach, EXIT. Das Buch. Der geheime Schatz

First published in 2024 in the United States and Canada by Puzzlewright Junior, an imprint of Sterling Publishing Co., Inc. First published in Germany as EXIT. Das Buch. Der geheime Schatz in 2019 by Franckh-Kosmos Verlags-GmbH & Co. KG.

ISBN 978-1-4549-5871-0

For information about custom editions, special sales, and premium purchases, please contact specialsales@unionsquareandco.com.

Printed in Slovakia

Lot #:
10 9 8 7 6 5 4 3 2 1

08/24

unionsquareandco.com

English translation: Collaborate Agency
Authors: Inka and Markus Brand, Anna and Mo Maybach
Illustrations: Burkhard Schulz / COMICON S.L. / Beroy + San Julian
English-language puzzle consultant: Francis Heaney

"The cave has to be around here somewhere!" I shouted to Anup. Anup had been my best friend since the very first day of first grade. "I'm pretty sure..." That's all I got out before I tripped on something and tumbled headfirst into a ditch filled with leaves from last fall. It's not very smart to look behind you while running forward – especially when there are rocks or trees in your way!

The leaves made a loud crunching noise as I emerged from them, blowing a dry leaf from the tip of my nose. Another one was stuck across my eye – I bet it looked very pirate-like! As I plucked it off, I noticed a small hole in the ground. It was right in front of me, hidden between the roots of a windswept fir tree. And there in the bushes was a tuft of hair. It was almost as red as mine.

"Great landing, Lucia!" Anup reached out his hand to me from the edge of the shallow trench and tried to hold back a laugh. That's what friends do – they don't laugh when something silly happens to the other, even if it's not always easy!

We were both looking for the mysterious Dragon's Cave. According to an old legend, it was somewhere in this forest. And the same legend claimed that inside the Dragon's Cave was a magic treasure!

Anup stared at me with wide eyes. "Did you just find the entrance to the cave?"

I shook my head. "No, only this." I pointed to the tuft of red fur.

"It's probably from a fox, and this is just a fox den." Anup sounded disappointed but helped me out of the ditch.

"But the cave must be somewhere around here... I just feel it." I plucked the last few leaves out of my hair buns. Then I sat beside Anup under a tree and carefully pulled the map from my backpack. It was hundreds of years old and crackled when I opened it up. Hopefully, this map would help us find the cave entrance – and the treasure.

Every time I touched the faded lines and traces of ink on it, I got goosebumps. It was a hot morning, but I could feel the tiny hairs between my freckles standing up.

I squinted at the sun in the bright blue sky that stretched over the lake and the hills like a tent. Every now and then, a few white clouds floated by, turning into cloud animals before dissolving again. It was only June, but it hadn't rained in weeks. It hadn't been this hot and dry for ages. It just had to be fate!

The lake's water level dropped low enough to allow entry into the mysterious Dragon's Cave only in the hottest summers; the rest of the time, it was underwater. Everyone in the area knew this. But no one really knew where the cave was. The treasure could be found only on one day every year: the summer solstice. It was the longest day of the year – and it was today!

But first, we had to find the entrance to the cave. I leaned over the map and read the ancient writing on it for the zillionth time:

> Follow the dragon, the ancient snake,
> guarding over the crystal lake.
> Past the oak grove where the rowan sways,
> it creeps along on both dark nights and days
> towards the rocks, where guardians, the Three,
> stand high upon the hillside free.
> But the treasure eludes you, from all kept at bay,
> 'til sun swallows deep waters
> and clouds' display.
> And only then, at the lofty gate,
> the siblings grant entry, don't hes...

Here, a piece of the map - and part of the words - was missing.

"The dragon *has* to be the rock at the bathing spot!" I exclaimed. Anup nodded in agreement.

"Now that the water's so shallow, the rock really does look like a dragon's head from up here. A dragon's head with a raised crest and flared nostrils." Anup pointed to the ridges and spikes in the rock that normally lay hidden below the water's surface. "And there are rowans around here!" he added. "Rowan" is the name for the type of tree with silvery bark that we were leaning against. Although some people call it "bird-berry" or "mountain-ash."

I knew this because Anup, who knows more about plants and animals than anybody else, had told me. And my mom, who knows everything about folklore and fairytales, said that in the old legends, the tree was magical.

I liked fairy tales. And the ancient words in them. I wrote down my favorite words in my ledger. "*Ledger*" is one of those special words, and it means a kind of notepad with lots of space for writing.

"And there are tons of rocks," said Anup, checking out the boulders between the trees.

I jumped up. We'd been sitting around for far too long. "Now we just need to find the right three rocks. As the map says: 'Towards the rocks, where guardians, the Three, stand high upon the hillside free.'"

"Can we just rest a minute?" grumbled Anup. I grabbed his hand and pulled him along behind me.

About an hour later, we ended up right back where we had started. We'd looked under and behind all the rocks that somehow stood in groups of three, but not a trace of a clue!

"If luck isn't on our side, we could search for the entrance forever and never find it, even if the three rocks on the map are super close," sighed Anup. "It's so annoying that your map is missing a piece. We don't even know where north and south are supposed to be."

Sure, he was right, but at least we had a map! Even if it wasn't complete, it had traveled through the ages and passed through many hands to reach us. That had to count for *something*, didn't it?

"If it were easy to find the treasure, it would have been gone long ago!" I said.

Anup shrugged. "We've been looking for hours and still haven't found anything."

That wasn't completely true. We had discovered several cracks in the rocks, two fox dens, and a caved-in passageway. A rusted bucket and a braided rope lay right in front of the passageway. Although the rope was old and green with moss, it still seemed strong enough, so I had taken it with me. I'd also taken a fishing hook I'd found wedged between the rocks on the lakeshore or the red string tangled in the bushes. It made a neat little ball of yarn when I rolled it up. *Who knows, this stuff might come in handy*, I had thought.

This would have been a decent haul on an ordinary day, but today was no ordinary day – it was the day of the solstice. And it was our only chance of finding the entrance to the cave and the treasure.

Anup took a sip from his canteen and pointed to the faded letters and lines that someone had drawn on the map a very long time ago. "So many people must have looked for the treasure before us. If no one has found it yet, we probably won't, either."

"You're not going to quit, are you?" I gasped in horror.

Then all of this would have been for nothing! I'd gone through the trouble of borrowing the treasure map from Mom... and her fancy jump rope, too. And I hadn't asked permission, either. It would be a shame to have nothing to show for it.

As long as I brought back the map and a treasure, I'm sure she wouldn't stay mad for long. Because she was just about the best mom in the world. Unfortunately, the map really belonged to the museum that Mom worked at. They had lots of old books and papers. Some were just plain; other books were fancy, decorated with silver and gemstones. But pretty much all of them looked tattered, had water damage, or had torn pages or covers.

These books wound up in Mom's workshop, where they waited to be dusted, cleansed of mold and dirt, and fixed. But in this case, it's not called "fixing" but "restoring." Don't ask me why. Grown-ups came up with that word. Adults often make things more complicated than they need to be. They say, *"It's complicated,"* which is just another word for "difficult," and not even a nice one.

"It's complicated," my mom and dad told me when they explained that they weren't "compatible" anymore, that they'd be splitting up but still be friends. I thought they were awesome together, but it didn't make any difference.

Ever since then, I've spent a lot of my time after school in Mom's workshop on the first floor of our crooked little house.

I loved the *"snap-crackle"* sound when I opened the brittle covers of the books, the smell of the old paper, and the swishing of the dusting brush. Sometimes I was allowed to help. When it came to the valuable manuscripts with gold lettering, colorful drawings, and squiggles, Mom only let me watch. But every now and then, she'd let me have one of the boxes that people in the neighborhood brought to her. Word had gotten around that she was into the history and stories of the area.

Most of the old books and papers were nothing special. Some were important because of the times they talked about, like the years during the *Cold War*. Only grown-ups could think up a whole new type of *war* like it was a new drink at a coffee shop. I found a lot of this stuff boring, but sometimes there was a real treasure among them. Or a map to a treasure. Or, to be more exact, to a treasure cave. And if we found the entrance to the Dragon's Cave today, we would surely find the dragon's treasure, too! That's what I thought.

What I *hoped*.

"I sure don't want to give up! It would be awesome if we found the treasure!" Anup kicked a clump of dirt out of the way. "But I don't know where else to look."

"The answer must be right here!" I tapped on the map. "We just can't see it!"

Anup sighed. "So, let's start over from the beginning: we just climbed up the hill from the dragon rock."

I nodded. "Yes, just like it says on the map: '*Past the oak grove where the rowan sways.*'"

"That's it, Lucia!" shouted Anup, laughing.

"That's *what?!*" I had no idea what he was talking about.

"There are rowans here. And fir trees. But there aren't any..." Instead of finishing his sentence, he spun me around in a circle.

Suddenly I understood. "No *oak* trees! There are no oaks here," I noticed.

We had been so sure that we had to go up the hill to the rowans that we never even thought about the other trees on the map.

Above us, a fluffy white cloud drifted by. At first, it looked like a fish. Then, the front part stretched out and made a head. The fins turned into wings. A dragon!

A gust of wind swirled the cloud around. Now, the dragon lay on its back.

I looked from the cloud to Anup, then from Anup to the map.

"This means," I thought out loud, "that we are on the wrong side!"

I ran my finger counterclockwise across the map, away from the dragon's head, in other words, to my left. There were a lot of trees there, too.

"Hey," I said, "are there any oaks on the other side of the lake?"

"Of course!" Anup jumped up. "Oaks and rowans. And this." He pointed to a drawing on the map, showing three rocks of different heights on the side of the lake opposite the dragon's head. "This could be *'the Three'* that will lead us to the entrance!"

Can you find the dragon rock on the map? Then grab a pen and take the same path as Lucia: follow the dotted line from the dragon's head to the trees, going counterclockwise. And from the trees, keep going to "the Three." Along the way, you will find some numbers to put into your decoding strip.

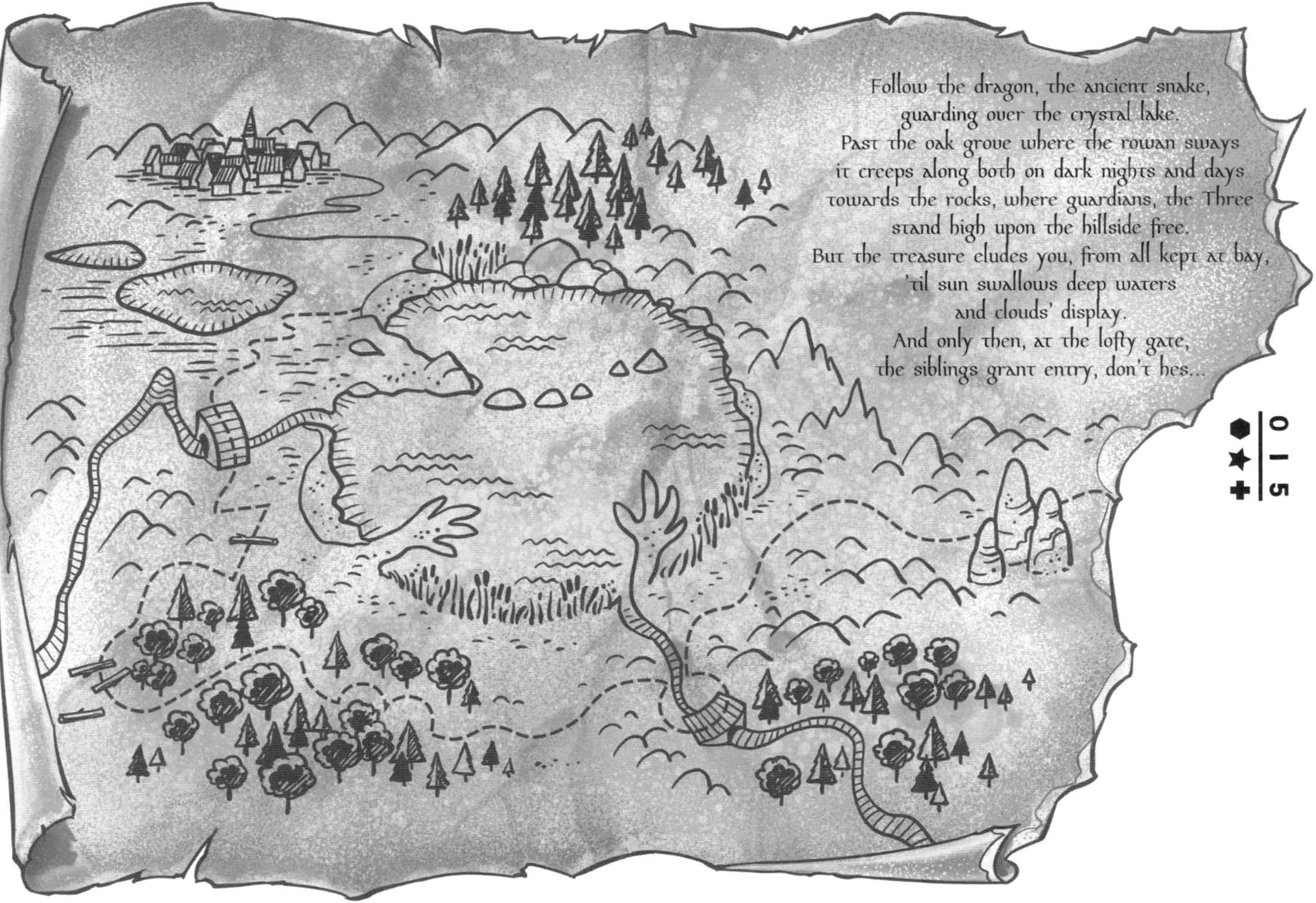
Follow the dragon, the ancient snake,
guarding over the crystal lake.
Past the oak grove where the rowan sways
it creeps along both on dark nights and days
towards the rocks, where guardians, the Three
stand high upon the hillside free.
But the treasure eludes you, from all kept at bay,
'til sun swallows deep waters
and clouds' display.
And only then, at the lofty gate,
the siblings grant entry, don't hes...

I felt a little weird standing in the middle of the vault. I was holding hands with Pierce and Anup, who were standing on my right and left. We had crossed out almost all the drawings and symbols on the walls, and all that was left was a picture of the siblings, also holding hands. Pierce had pointed out that they were standing in the middle of a circle. And since the vault was also round, Anup had come up with the idea that we should stand in the middle and do the same. I sighed. We must have been wrong. Frustrated, I shifted my weight, leaned my head back, closed my eyes for a moment – and immediately snapped them open again.

"Stop squirming, Lucia," Pierce grumbled, holding my hand tighter so I wouldn't fall backwards. "Or you'll end up with a bruise instead of the treasure."

"*Pfft*!" I huffed, but I couldn't pretend to be mad any longer. I nodded my head towards the ceiling. "There, there it is!"

Pierce and Anup flung their heads back. Right above us, on the ceiling, we saw a painted circle. A circle you could only see if you stood right in the middle and leaned way back. From it, rays shone like sunbeams. One of the rays was longer than the others.

It pointed to the passageway to my left, the one with the rainbow above it.

"Hooray!" I laughed. "We've solved the riddle, that's where we need to go from here!"

"Why didn't we see it straight away?" Anup scratched his head.

But as soon as we let go of each other and stepped into the center, it vanished again.

"Light and shadow!" Pierce called out like he understood what was going on. "The symbol of the light isn't drawn on; it's cut into the stone. That's why you can only see it when it casts a shadow. And you have to stand at just the right angle!"

"OK, let's go!" ordered Anup and ran into the passageway, followed by Pierce.

Lost in thought, I hurried after them. Didn't they realize what this meant? Only the three of us together could have figured out the answer!

Obviously, they didn't, because Anup and Pierce zoomed past me down the slope as if they were in a contest. It got steeper and steeper, and the water dripping from the walls made the ground slippery. And all of a sudden, Anup started skidding on the wet rock and crashed into Pierce. Pierce tried to catch Anup and landed next to him on the muddy ground.

They both tried hard to hold on to the walls, but in vain, and they slid through the mud towards the next bend. I leaped forward but grasped at nothing, tripping and also losing my balance.

"Ouch!" I landed hard on my butt and continued sliding out of control. No matter how hard I tried to find something to hold onto, I just went faster and faster. I was speeding forward like on a water slide. Somewhere in front of me, I heard Anup and Pierce yelling. My heart was beating like crazy. Then I whooshed around one final bend and ended up flying through the air.

Another cave, I realized, with a quiet, deep lake and a waterfall running into it on the opposite side. Then I hit the floor, softer than I thought I would.

"*Urgh!*" Pierce, who I had landed on, groaned and gasped for air.

I crawled to the side. "I'm sorry – are you OK?"

"I'm fine! At least we ended up here and not over *there*."

He pointed ahead to where the rock fell away into the water. The color was amazing – almost turquoise. But no matter how pretty it looked, I really didn't feel like swimming in it.

Luckily, a flat rock was sticking out of the water about a yard from us. It had drawings and symbols carved into the top.

At its center, there was a glow, and it was as if the glow was calling out to me.

I got up and took off as fast as I could. "Lucia, what are you doing?" Pierce yelled, but I kept running. And then I jumped.

Seconds later, I held the third and final piece of the amulet in my hand. Even in the dimly lit cave, it glittered and shimmered – I couldn't begin to imagine what it would look like with the sun shining on the translucent gemstone in the middle.

I turned to Pierce and Anup and showed them what I'd found. Anup didn't hesitate for long. With a proud grin he landed right next to me. Pierce, who was looking at the water nervously, followed soon after him. "I hope you know where to go from here?"

"We'll swim if we have to," Anup said coolly, pulling out his amulet piece and holding it next to mine. The gemstones seemed to shine twice as bright as the faint light that found its way into the cave from somewhere high above us.

Pierce mumbled something that sounded like "when pigs fly."

Anup nudged him. "Hold yours next to ours. Remember, all three of our amulets fit together to make one piece!"

As soon as Pierce held his amulet piece next to Anup's and mine, the rays of light merged. It was like the kaleidoscope my parents and I had made from pieces of mirror and glass beads.

"I thought so," Anup said, more to himself than to us. Then he pointed to the spot on the rock from where I had removed the amulet. "All three pieces belong there."

Perplexed, Pierce and I leaned over it. I looked at the hollow. It was decorated with a pattern of squiggles and curls and was big enough to fit all three pieces.

Pierce squatted down. "And if we put the amulet pieces in here, will they show us the treasure?" he asked.

"At least they'll show us where to go from here." Anup sounded totally sure. "The treasure could be anywhere." He pointed into the water.

"There?" squeaked Pierce. "You mean in the water?"

"Of *course* in the water!" Anup laughed. "Just like the legend says: the siblings threw behind them all they had. And the king tried to gather it up as the water came rushing in."

Pierce took a deep breath. "At least we each have a gemstone," he muttered. "So let's do this. I want to go home and show my father what I've found."

Anup turned to me and asked, "Any idea which order we have to put the amulets into the rock, Lucia?"

"Me? Why me?" I asked.

"Because you're our combo lock expert. And the Guardian of the Light."

Continue reading on the next page.

Lucia, Pierce and Anup need your help. Cut out the amulet on the next page around the outer line. Always cut and fold carefully or ask an adult to help you.
Start at 1. Fold the amulet along the line and in the direction the arrow points, so you can no longer see the pattern. Then cut along all of the dotted lines with this symbol: 🔒

Continue at 2. Again, fold the paper in the direction of the arrow. This time, you need to cut along the dotted lines with the symbol: 🔑

Last, follow the arrow to fold the whole piece of paper along the line indicated by the number 3. Look for this symbol to cut out another piece: ✋

Now your amulet is ready for the next step! Look for the second piece in Lucia's Secret Book and follow the instructions there. If you made a mistake when cutting out your amulet, you can find another one on page 025.

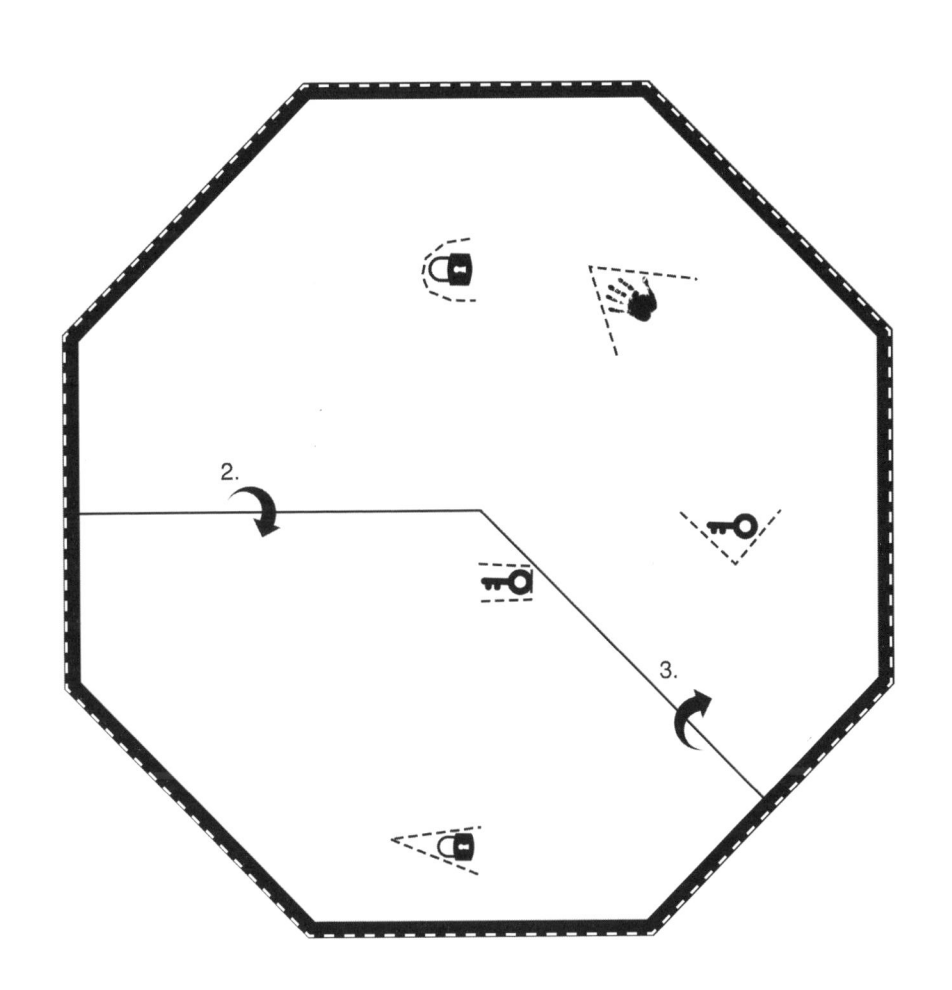

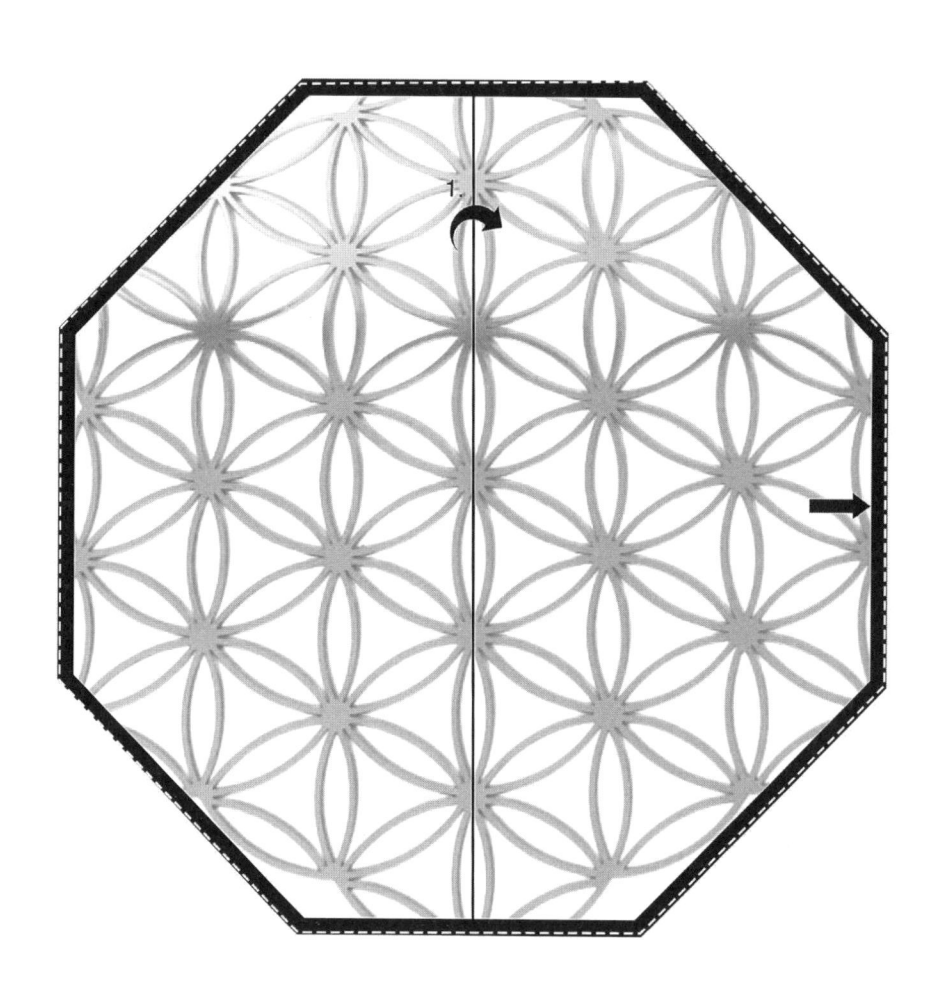

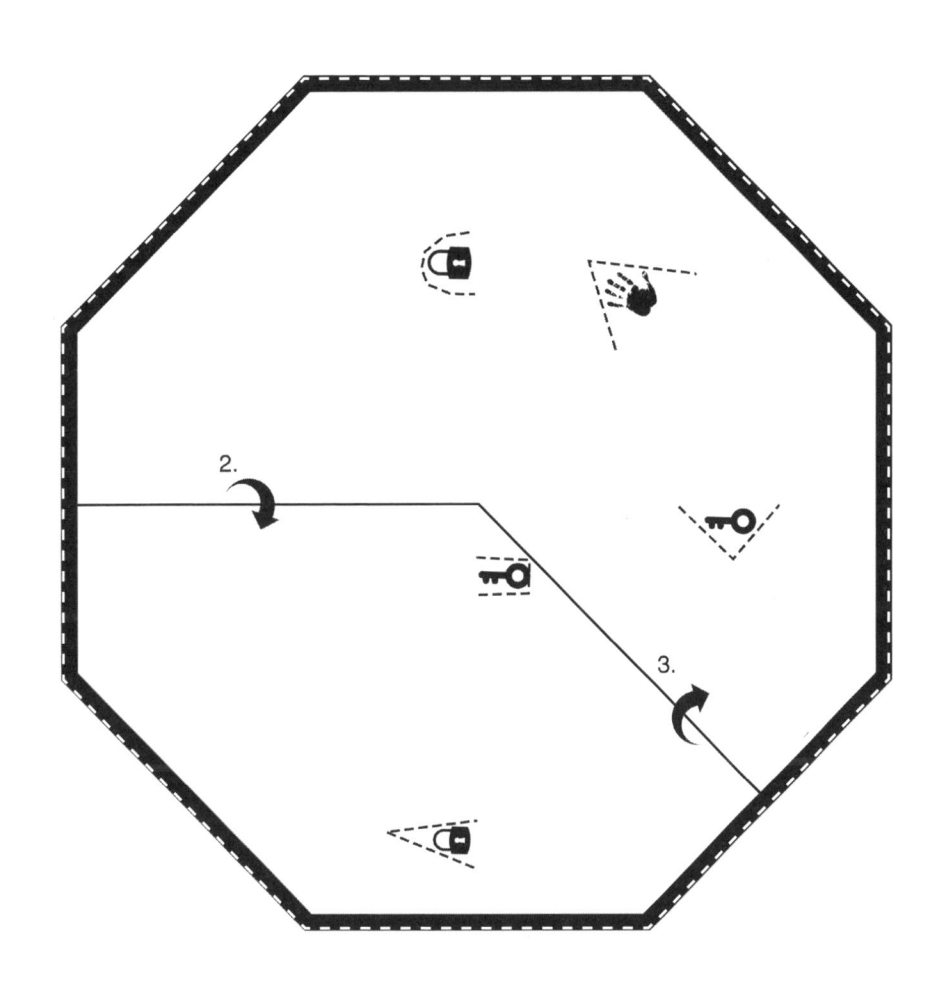

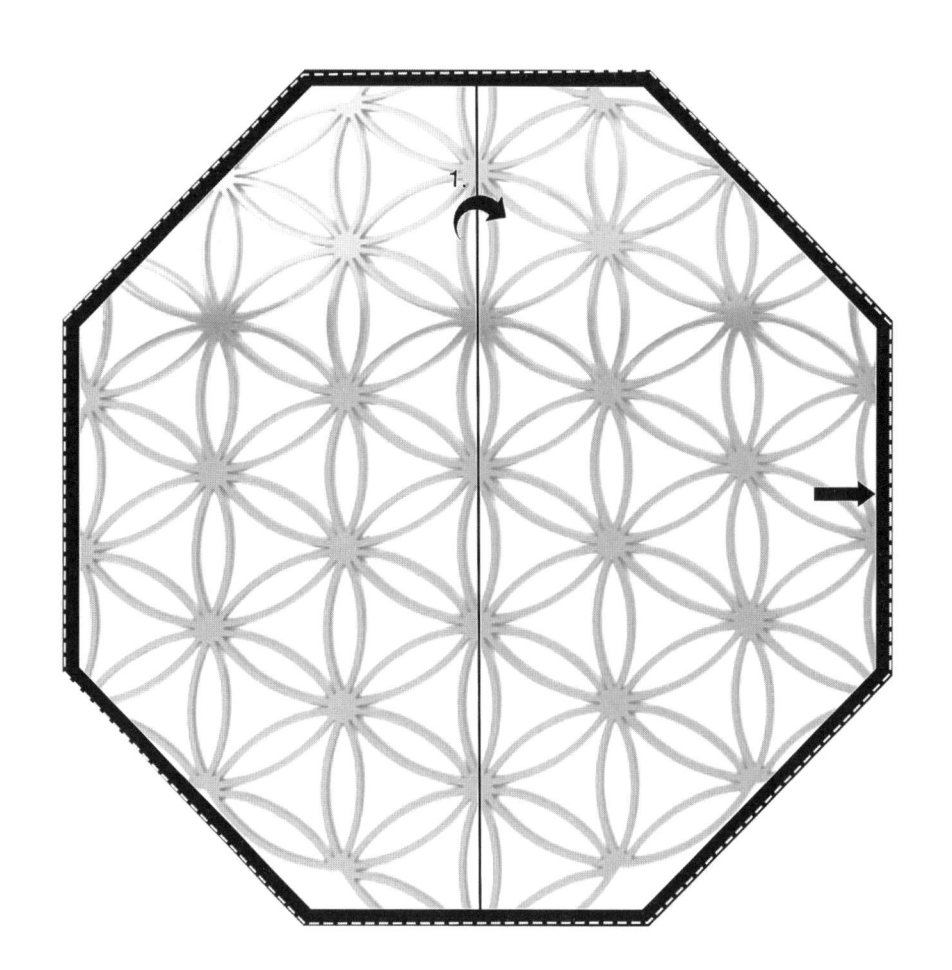

The steps in the chamber below the throne spiraled down into complete darkness. We bent over them. "Of all places, it has to continue there?" muttered Anup.

And even Pierce agreed. "It's pretty dark and narrow!"

I shuddered. I could handle darkness. Not so much confined spaces.

Pierce switched on his flashlight. "I'll lead the way!" Anup and I remained silent, and he grinned sneakily. "Or are you afraid I'll find more treasures?"

I shrugged. "You can go ahead, but we should stay together." Then I turned to Anup. "Agreed?"

Anup nodded. "There must be a reason why the cave is leading us this way. Let's get moving."

"The cave!" Pierce laughed as he swung his legs over the edge of the throne. "You make it sound like it has a mind of its own."

Anup let me go first. "Who knows," he whispered. "I'm not sure *what* to believe anymore."

I couldn't have said it better myself. No matter how much we thought we knew about the dragon legend, the cave seemed to have its own story to tell...

I gritted my teeth. Walking down a narrow spiral staircase in the dark wasn't exactly one of my favorite things to do. Luckily Pierce was running ahead, so he didn't hear when Anup asked softly, "Are you OK?" I nodded silently and continued fumbling my way forward. At least the steps were getting wider.

I was about to breathe a sigh of relief when Pierce shouted from ahead, "Be careful, the rock face is receding from the steps. Don't fall into the gap."

A gap? What? I pulled my cell phone out of my pocket and shined the light to my right. Sure enough, the crack was widening. But you couldn't see all the way to the bottom! How far down did it go?

I shuddered and almost ran into Pierce, who suddenly stopped.

"We've got a problem," he said. "I'm standing on the last step."

"We're at the bottom?" I was ecstatic. "Finally!"

"Not quite," he replied. "The last part of the stairs is missing."

"Excuse me?" I asked, horrified.

He stepped aside so I could see for myself. Anup, who was clutching the central pillar as I was, peeked over my shoulder. The last steps of the spiral staircase were gone.

Perhaps there had been an earthquake, or maybe they'd been flushed out by water? There was no way of knowing.

But about two yards below us, the broken fragments now rose like jagged peaks from an inky black pond. Its surface rippled as if something was swimming around in it.

Anup flicked the beam of his flashlight around the chamber. Something blue reflected back from one of the far walls. It was maybe three yards from us, on the other side of the round shaft. Anup stepped next to Pierce and knelt down.

"You don't really want to go down there, do you?" Pierce asked.

But Anup was already carefully shimmying down to the first ledge just below the last step. Circles formed on the water's surface, but Anup focused only on the blue glow. Balancing carefully on the broken, jagged remains of the steps jutting out of the pond, he made his way towards it.

I squinted. The glow came from a translucent, watery blue gemstone. It was set in metal that was twisted into a nine. Or a six. Or part of the symbols we kept discovering on the cave walls.

"This is the second part of the amulet," I whispered excitedly. "You're almost there, Anup!"

Almost immediately, I wished I hadn't spoken, because when Anup looked over his shoulder to smile at me, he twisted his ankle. It felt like slow motion as I watched him stumble.

My scream echoed off the walls. I shoved my cell phone into Pierce's hand and jumped down onto the second broken section of stairs. I grabbed my best friend and pulled him back, away from the dark water. We hit the back wall of the shaft hard. Anup looked at me, his eyes wide with shock.

"Why did you do that?" Anup asked.

"Sorry," I mumbled. "You tripped, and I thought –" I broke off sheepishly. I knew how much Anup hated the fact that everyone always thought he needed help.

But he just grinned. "It wasn't necessary, but thank you." Then he reached past me and fished the piece of jewelry out of a hollow in the rock. We were bending over the amulet in amazement when Pierce also jumped down onto the first broken step in the water.

"Are you crazy?" I shouted. "How are we supposed to get up now?"

Pierce rolled his eyes. "And how am I supposed to help you from up there? There's nothing to hold on to. At least I can give you a leg up from here." He handed my cell phone back to me.

Anup stared at him. "And how are you going to get back up there?"

Pierce shrugged. "Jump and pull myself up?" he suggested. "I should be able to make it."

My first thought was to start arguing with him. But then I realized he really thought it was the best option for all three of us. Looking around, I noticed a massive snout sticking out of the shaft wall above us. Two eyes glowed on either side of it.

Pierce followed my gaze. "The dragon!" He ducked down and Anup and I huddled beside him.

But apart from the splashing of the water, there was not a sound to be heard. No hissing, no fiery breath, no rumbling. Hesitantly, I raised my head and burst out laughing. What we had thought were two eyes above a dragon's mouth turned out to be nothing more than two passages to the right and left of the rocky outcrop. From the tunnels' openings gleamed the same glowing algae we had seen in the cave with the raft. But they were too far above us to reach. I slowly stood up. What we needed now was my mom's jump rope. Maybe we could throw it over the ledge... but which of the two entrances was the right one?

I sighed, turned around, and did a double-take. This time there really *was* a snout sticking out of the water in front of me. A tiny snout. The pale little face that came with it turned to the side as if to ask, *"Why are you making such a racket?"*

Small feet paddled in the water, and a longish body, shimmering pink in the light, wriggled back and forth. Then another tiny snout appeared.

"How cute!" Curious, Anup crouched down.

Pierce wrinkled his nose. "You think water snakes are cute?"

"They're not snakes!" Anup cautiously held out his hand. "They're cave salamanders."

Pierce looked unrelieved. "How is that better than snakes?"

The little critters that had been paddling around Anup's fingers lifted their heads out of the water. Maybe it was just a coincidence, but I thought they looked pretty annoyed. They also looked like something else...

"Hey!" I shouted. "Maybe it's the salamanders' fault that everyone thinks there are dragons in the cave? Look at that!"

I pointed into the water. Next to their heads, the tiny animals had small, fluttering tufts that were probably gills, but in the shape of tiny wings.

"You're right!" Anup was excited. "They really do look like newly hatched baby dragons!"

"But they aren't, are they?" Pierce said hesitantly. "So there are no dragons here, and maybe no treasure, either?"

"Who knows?" I shrugged. "We've already found two amulet pieces! There must be more!"

"Well, then," Pierce suggested, "we should go back and find another way." He stood under the step we had jumped down from and joined his hands together.

"Who should I help up first?"

I wrinkled my nose in thought. "No one. If you ask me, that's where we need to go." I pointed to the two holes next to the ledge above us.

Anup nodded. "Yeah, I think so too. The only question is: right or left? And how do we get up there?"

"Umm..." Pierce pointed behind us to where the salamanders were dancing in the water. "Are those weird mini dragons trying to tell us something?"

Anup and I turned around in surprise. Sure enough, there was a dark, wet, egg-shaped stone stuck between the sharp-edged fragments the salamanders were swimming around. When we shined a light on it, we could see scales glistening.

I reached for it hesitantly. No, it wasn't a rock. It was an egg! A dragon's egg, perhaps? It felt rough and cold but quickly warmed up under my fingers. When I pulled it out, I realized that it wasn't a real egg, but some kind of metal jewelry box. It made a crunching sound as I turned the two pieces against each other, and the salamanders disappeared.

Had the noise frightened them or had their mission been accomplished? Had they actually given us a clue?

"What is it?" Pierce asked.

I removed the lid and took out the old parchment that was inside the box. "A sheet of paper," I said, carefully unrolling it. "Probably another riddle."

Anup laughed. "What *else* could it be? What's it about this time?"

"About gems and the king?" I guessed, pointing to the drawings on the page, surrounded by lines and arrows.

"There's something on the back, too!" Pierce took the parchment from my hand and turned it over. There were lines and parts of drawings, too, strangely scattered all over the page.

"Maybe we need to roll or fold the paper in some way," Anup suggested.

Cautiously, Pierce folded one part of the sheet, then another. "Not in *any* way." He sighed. "But exactly according to the instructions!"

Now it's your turn: cut out the parchment and follow the instructions carefully to fold the picture of the king and cross out any gems he can no longer see.

The ancient legend of the greedy king

For many years, the king had been searching the cave for gems. One day, he lost all of his strength and hunkered down on the ground, right next to all his gems.

Now fold this top section down along the black line by the number 1.

1.

2.

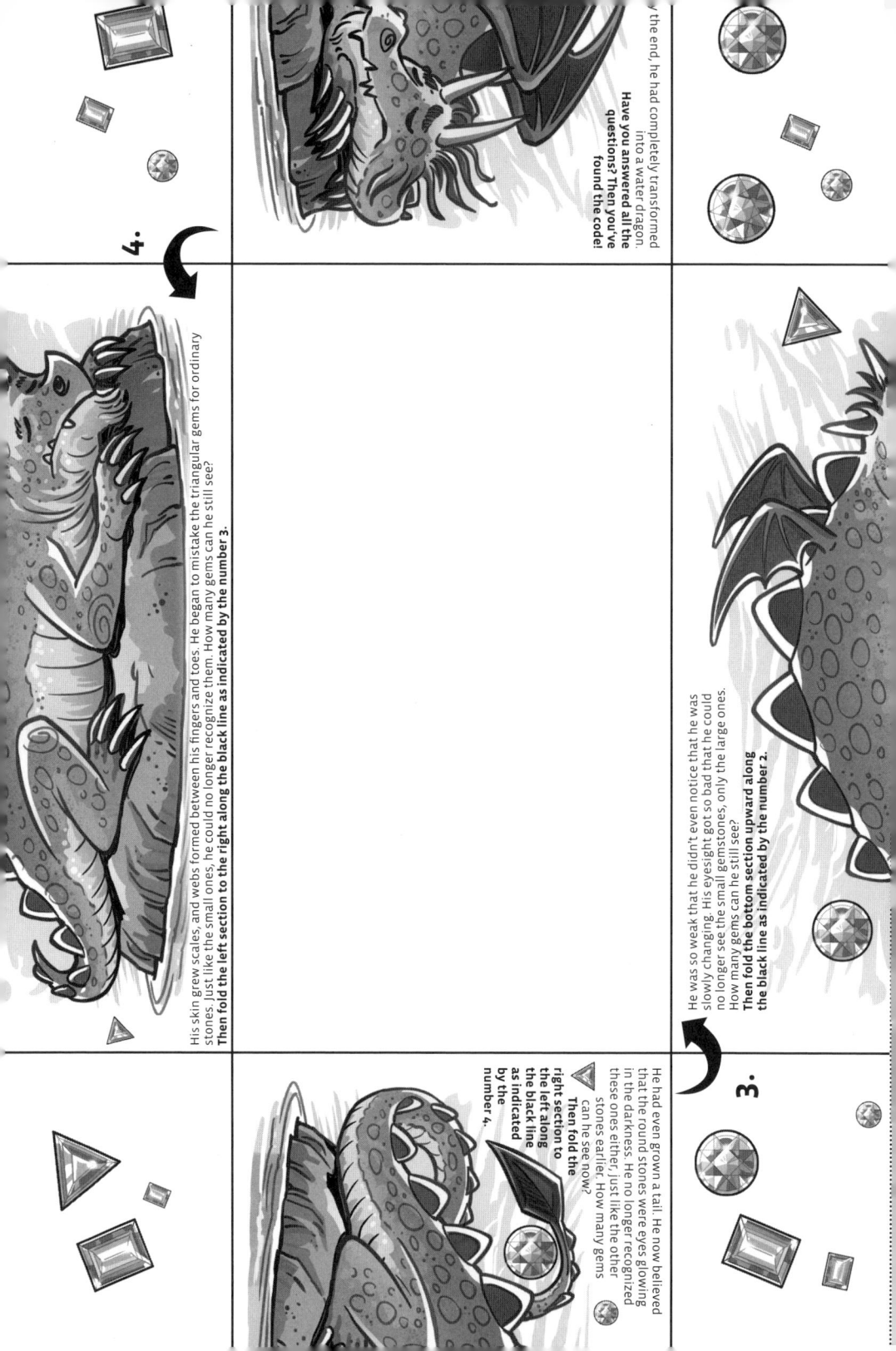

the end, he had completely transformed into a water dragon. **Have you answered all the questions? Then you've found the code!**

4.

His skin grew scales, and webs formed between his fingers and toes. He began to mistake the triangular gems for ordinary stones. Just like the small ones, he could no longer recognize them. How many gems can he still see? **Then fold the left section to the right along the black line as indicated by the number 3.**

He was so weak that he didn't even notice that he was slowly changing. His eyesight got so bad that he could no longer see the small gemstones, only the large ones. How many gems can he still see? **Then fold the bottom section upward along the black line as indicated by the number 2.**

3.

He had even grown a tail. He now believed that the round stones were eyes glowing in the darkness. He no longer recognized these ones either, just like the other stones earlier. How many gems can he see now? **Then fold the right section to the left along the black line as indicated by the number 4.**

We had to turn the amulets back and forth a few times until they connected together perfectly and fit into the rock. The metal settings faced outward, while the three gems lay close together on the inside. We had just taken a step back when they caught the last faint rays of the setting sun. There was a low, distant rumble, and suddenly the cave was bathed in all the colors of the rainbow. The dazzling beam from our amulets spread out and, like a bridge of light, gently curved and pointed at the waterfall.

But wait – the light didn't stop at the waterfall. No, the beam continued through the babbling, cascading water. It illuminated a semicircular opening behind it.

The sight almost took my breath away. "The exit is through the waterfall. How awesome is that?"

"Not at all," Pierce disagreed and took his amulet piece. Immediately, the bridge of light disappeared, and there was a muffled bang as if someone had slammed a door.

Anup blinked in the direction of the waterfall. "Put it back, Pierce. The exit's gone."

"Nonsense!" Pierce pocketed his amulet piece. "It's not gone. We know where it is now. Now we just have to get there. Preferably around the outside."

"No." I thought of the loud bang and the legend and shook my head. "The exit only opens when all three amulets are here. They're like a key, and the hollow in the rock is the lock."

Pierce stared at me. "You want us to leave them here? The only valuable thing we found?"

I nodded.

Pierce clenched his fists. "That's not fair!" He punched his own thigh in frustration and stared into the water. "I can't leave without at least taking a diamond or something!" Then he collapsed to the ground. "I have to take *something* back to my father, otherwise it was all for nothing!"

Anup and I exchanged a surprised look.

Then Anup sat down next to Pierce. "If it's so important to you," he said, "jump into the water and dive for the gems. You can keep whatever you find."

"But," I added, crouching down beside them, "you should hurry. When the sun goes down, we'll be stuck here for who knows how long."

"I can't!" Pierce shook his head angrily. "I can't swim."

"What?" Well, that was a surprise. But it explained why he never showed up at the pool for gym class.

I gently tugged at his sleeve. "Why can't you swim?"

Pierce sighed. "Because my dad and granddad can't either." He hunched his shoulders up to his ears. "Mom promised to teach me," he groaned angrily. "But then she just had to go! She said she had to go somewhere she could do more. Where she could be more than just... well, Dad's wife and Grandpa's daughter. More than my mother." He took a shaky breath. "And things haven't been right at home since."

I put my hand on his arm. On the other side, Anup moved closer to him. "But why do you need a gemstone for that?" he asked quietly.

Pierce choked. "To prove to my father that I'm good for something? He used to play soccer with me. Now he just can't be bothered. He just sits on the couch after work. He's working two jobs now because he lost his regular one. And I thought if I brought him back a gem, it might cheer him up!" He looked from Anup to me. "Besides, we could sell it and maybe go on vacation again or do some fun things!"

"I have an idea!" Anup stood up. "What if we just come back here? Tomorrow or the day after. We've solved all the puzzles. We know the routes through the caves!"

I nodded. "And maybe," I said, "we can even get in through the waterfall exit. It would be a shortcut."

"And when we get back here," Anup turned to Pierce, "I'll dive to get a gem for you."

"You'd *do* that?" asked Pierce.

"Of course!" Anup grinned. "Because first of all, you're not as dumb as I thought..."

"And secondly," I took over, "we're kinda a team now, aren't we?"

Pierce looked at us. Very slowly his face broke into a smile. "All right." He nodded and put his amulet back into the rock.

Instantly, the light bridge reappeared, and the gate opened. But we still had a problem: Pierce couldn't swim, and we had to get through the water somehow. But luckily, I had an idea. A really crazy Lucia idea!

Continue reading on page 107.

Anup and I shifted into high gear to
reach Pierce as quickly as possible. First,
we squeezed through the narrow space
between two pillars, then ducked under eight
overhanging stalactites. And suddenly we found ourselves in a
brightly lit chamber right inside the stalactite cave! All around
us, the stalagmites and stalactites formed an arch.

In the center of the chamber was a long, rectangular rock
that looked like a table. On a ledge behind it, a tall, almost
round block of stone had been carved into a seat. It had a high
backrest behind it etched with patterns. They looked like
stalactites joining together. Small round, oval, and angular
patterns had been chiseled into the rock between the peaks.
They were shaped like gems and painted red, yellow, blue,
and green. Though the colors were faded, and the backrest
was brittle, the rock chair still looked like a throne. A throne
waiting for its king. Next to the stone table, a stalactite from
the ceiling and a stalagmite from the floor merged into one
pillar. There was a flash of amber where they met.

I looked up. The light had to come from somewhere. And
yes, there above us in the dome of rock were shafts of light
arranged in a circle.

Anup also looked up at them. "The light, the chair, the table... everything looks like it was designed with a purpose."

"Maybe," I whispered back, "this is the throne room of the Guardian of the Mountains."

Anup and I were mesmerized by the magic of this chamber among the stalactites, but Pierce was already busy with something else. To my horror, I saw that he had planted one foot on the pillar next to the rock table and was yanking on something with all his might. Metal crunched against stone.

"Stop!" Anup shouted. "What are you doing?"

Pierce had grabbed a finely forged chain to pull out the piece of jewelry stuck between the stalagmites and stalactites. Could this be the third part of the amulet? The stone in the center glowed almost golden.

"It must be part of the treasure," Pierce panted. "And it's mine! I saw it first!"

"Are you crazy? You mustn't force it out!"

I tried to grab Pierce's arm, but he turned away and continued to pull. "How else am I going to get it?" he growled. "It's stuck in this column and I have to break it to get it out!"

"No way!" I trembled. *No one must destroy anything to get to the amulet*, I thought. *Otherwise, we would be no better than the greedy king in the legend!*

I threw my arms around Pierce and tried to drag him away. But he pushed me aside.

"What's the big idea, pushing Lucia like that?" Anup shoved Pierce so hard that he staggered backward a few steps.

Pierce spun around and clenched his fists in anger. Anup pumped his arms as well.

"Have you two lost your minds? Cut it out!" I put two fingers into my mouth and whistled. The sound pierced the silence of the cave and echoed back to us. Pierce and Anup froze and looked at me, startled. There was a groan. Then a loud crunching and rumbling. "Wh... What was that?" stammered Pierce.

"The pillar! It moved!" Anup pointed to the column with the amulet lodged inside. True, it had shifted slightly.

"Whistle once more," Pierce urged me.

I did. And again, with a loud rumble, the stalagmite and the stalactite moved a tiny bit. The third time nothing happened. I was about to whistle a fourth time when Anup stopped me.

"Wait!" he warned. "I don't think whistling is enough." He had been looking at the back of the throne the whole time,

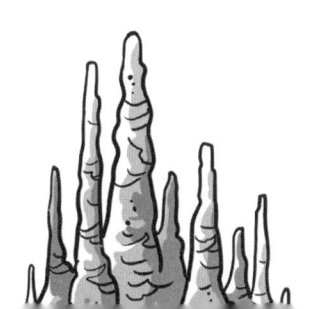

but now he pointed at the chiseled lines and designs. "Doesn't that look like musical notes?" he asked. "You know, like a tune. Can you whistle it, Lucia?"

I gave it a shot, using what I'd learned during music classes to read the notes. After a few misses, I managed to hit the right melody. The groaning and rumbling began again, rock scraping against rock. The stalagmite, the table, and the throne seemed to stand on a slab of rock that was slowly rotating by means of a hidden mechanism. The sections of the column slid apart, and the amulet clattered to the ground. "Mine!" Pierce quickly shouted, bending down to grab it, but Anup stepped on it before he could.

"Hey, I saw it first!" Pierce's eyes narrowed. I shoved my hands into my hips. "If I discover a cave full of gems," I asked Pierce slowly, "before Anup or you, will all the gems be mine?" For a moment Pierce was silent, uncertain. He looked at the amulet chain that was sticking out from under Anup's foot. "But you *haven't* found a treasure cave," he grumbled. "And I have found this amulet."

Anup and I exchanged a glance. I gave in. "If you want it bad enough, you can have it."

"But whatever else Lucia and I discover," Anup said as he released the amulet, "we won't share it with you."

Pierce paused. He looked back and forth between Anup, me, and the amulet and seemed to be mulling over our words.

Suddenly I had a thought: what if he didn't care so much about the amulet? What if his family needed money? Had he left with his grandfather's part of the map to help his father and grandpa?

"OK, I have a suggestion." I put my hand on Anup's, hoping he would understand. "How about we divide everything we find in the Dragon's Cave by three from now on?"

Anup frowned.

Pierce hesitantly pointed to the amulet, wondering, "What about this?"

I shrugged. "There should be three of them. Just keep this one."

Since we had one part of the amulet, it wasn't unlikely that we would find the other two on our way. What would happen then was anyone's guess. Probably something magical, I hoped. But for now, we had to keep going – the three of us, together.

Pierce put the amulet piece in his pocket and covered it with his hand. Anup turned in a circle, searching. "What now? Where to?" His voice echoed off the walls. "*To - to - to...*"
it whispered to us.

Well, that was the question. I didn't have the answer.
I was starting to feel a little exhausted. How long had we
been walking?

I ran to the stone throne to rest for a moment. But there was
no seat there. It must have moved sideways with the pillar.
Surprised, I leaned forward to find a black hole gaping in
front of me. And then I spotted some steps!

**Lucia has found a way forward. And so can you! On the
inner flap of the back cover of this book, you'll find the
cave. Start by cutting off the flap, then cut along the
dotted lines on the back. Don't you think it's funny how
the cut-out spikes look like stalagmites and stalactites?
The yellow lines will help you place them correctly on
the side with the gems.**

**If you've done everything correctly, you may notice
some gemstones wedged between the tips of the new
stalactites and stalagmites. But how can you use those
gems to find a three-digit code? Take another look at
the back of the cave. It might help you find it...**

"So?" Pierce wanted to know what we'd figured out as Anup and I high-fived over the maps we'd laid out next to each other.

We had both identified the same thing: the three symbols indicating the passage we had to take.

"It's the one with the DRAGON, the tree and the MAN, right?" Anup asked.

I nodded. "I should have guessed that the dragon symbol was one of them." I stuffed my precious Book of Legends and my other things into my backpack. "Let's go!"

Pierce hesitated. "And you're absolutely sure?"

"Just trust us," Anup said.

"Trust you?! Dangit, just *hold on* a minute!" Pierce snatched at the two map pieces Anup was holding. I tried to stop him, but he'd already managed to grab one of the corners. The ripping sound stopped Anup and me in our tracks. Pierce was holding a small scrap of paper in his hand.

"Have you lost it?" I cried, taking a closer look at the maps. Luckily, he hadn't managed to get his hands on Mom's map, only his grandpa's. "They're super valuable!"

Pierce acted unimpressed. "So what? They show us how to get out, don't they? So stop fussing, Princess!"

I folded up Mom's map, put it in my backpack for safekeeping, and shot Pierce an angry look. "*Princess?*"

Pierce was sneering at me now. "I thought you didn't want me to call you a witch anymore. Although, strictly speaking, what we agreed is no longer valid. After all, you didn't get me out of here. That means I can still call you whatever I want." He turned to Anup with a smug look. "How about it, Wobbles? Why don't you convince your copperhead friend to give me the two maps? Then I'll take care of things."

Anup looked at Pierce but didn't move. "You wish." Calmly, he nudged me into the correct tunnel. "You may have an idea which direction to go, but if you want to get out of the cave, you'll still need us," he called over his shoulder. "So you better be nice to us, otherwise we might just lose you down here!"

Pierce remained silent. Anup seemed to have taken him by surprise. It was several seconds before I heard Pierce's hesitant footsteps. And I could also hear Anup limping noticeably. He always limped when he was upset.

But if anyone was going to find their way around the Dragon's Cave, it was him and me. We knew the legend of the cave by heart and had pored over the map for ages. And in that moment, I wouldn't have minded if we lost Pierce somewhere!

After a few yards, we were in total darkness. Luckily, Pierce had also brought a flashlight with him. It was a really big one that belonged to his grandpa. With two flashlights and two cell phones, we were well equipped, I thought.

The path led us deeper into the mountain and slightly downhill, sometimes to the right, sometimes to the left. There had been no forks so far, but who knew what lay ahead? With some relief, I remembered the small ball of red string I had pocketed earlier in the forest. It might come in handy here, I figured. After all, anyone who is interested in fairy tales or legends knows how important it is to keep track of which turns you take. How else would you find your way back? And since my sense of direction was pretty good, even underground, I had a feeling we were headed for the entrance. Which happened to be the closest exit. Hopefully the drought of the last few weeks had made it usable! Otherwise, our great plan would be ruined. Or rather: Pierce's great plan.

Because I had no intention of leaving the Dragon's Cave again so soon. Not now that we had finally found it. And certainly not today, the only day we could possibly find the treasure! I turned to Anup and asked in a low voice, "Do you still have Pierce's map?

"Yeah, why?"

"Let me see it." I opened it and held it in front of me, shielding my phone. If the flashlight app worked, surely the photo app would. I launched it and took a picture. The flash lit up the narrow passage.

"What are you doing up there?" asked Pierce.

I quickly handed Pierce's part of the map back to Anup. "We're shining a light to see where we're going," I lied, chuckling to myself.

Now that Anup and I had the information from Pierce's map, we were no longer dependent on him. As far as I was concerned, he could go home when we reached the entrance. I had other plans!

Feeling quite pleased with myself, I continued walking and fiddled with my phone. While I was taking the pictures, the light from my cell phone's flashlight had turned off, but Anup's flashlight behind me was bright enough. Or so I thought, until I tripped over a rock and stumbled. Rats! I managed to steady myself and reactivated my flashlight. Good thing I did, or I would have taken another tumble – a big one! Because the passage came to an abrupt end just a few inches from the tips of my toes. Beyond the rock I'd stumbled over, the ground dropped steeply, revealing a descent into a deep cavern.

I heard Anup gasp in alarm.

"What are you guys doing?" Pierce asked as he came up beside us. He gulped when he saw the drop. "Whoa, that was close!" Our flashlights barely illuminated the ground, but we could see the glittering sharp edges of larger and smaller boulders below us.

"Is that... Is this... Is this the treasure cave? And is that the *gold* down there?" Pierce leaned forward eagerly.

Anup put a hand on his shoulder and held him back. "No, that's not the treasure. The stones down there are damp, that's why they glisten in the light."

"Damp?" Pierce wrinkled his nose. "I thought with the drought, there was no water left here!"

I shook my head. Pierce had obviously only half listened when we had learned about the dragon legend in class. "Just because the entrances aren't flooded doesn't mean all the caves are dry," I explained. "After all, some are lower than the lake outside!" I peeked over the edge where I could see shadows dancing back and forth. I pointed to the left. "Do you see that?" A narrow path led down the side of the rock face into the cave. Determined, I felt my way forward. "Careful, the rocks here might be damp and slippery."

I shot Anup a quick glance. "I'll go first, then Anup, and you last, Pierce."

"What? Why?" Pierce obviously wanted to argue again. But I certainly wasn't going to tell him why: if Anup stumbled along the narrow, uneven corridor leading down into the cave, it was better if he had someone in front of him and someone behind him to hold on to.

"Shut up and just *do it!*" I hissed.

For a moment it looked like Pierce was going to object when Anup shook out his right leg, the shorter one, to stabilize himself.

And, unbelievably, Pierce seemed to understand what was going on. He let Anup go ahead.

Step by step, we edged forward on the narrow, steep path along the rock face. Somewhere, something was dripping, and we could hear the frantic pitter-patter of small feet. I didn't want to know what creatures were trying to get away from us. According to the legend, there were dragons in the cave. But no one had written anything about how big they were.

If I were a dragon, I wouldn't be very pleased if some humans just wandered into my home. Hopefully, the dragons were less aggressive than the fire ants!

Continue reading on page 091. But don't forget to write the words in capital letters next to the corresponding symbols in Lucia's Secret Book.

"I was right!" Elated, I jumped up and down.

We had removed all the stones from the wall and swapped and rotated them until all the symbols on them matched those on the slab in the floor. As soon as we did, they clicked into place.

"It's like a combination lock, amazing!" I exclaimed.

"*You're* amazing." Anup beamed at me as the bars sank into the floor and the sides of the rock with a clatter.

"I agree." Pierce patted me on the shoulder and ushered us to the other side of the corridor. "Now, hurry up! We don't want that thing to close again!"

As if on cue, all the iron bars rumbled back into place.
I leaped forward.

Pierce sighed. "The siblings are really playing it safe. They keep blocking our way back."

But no matter how hard he tried to look grim, even he was enjoying our adventure by now.

We were making good progress. The passage was still wide, high, and well-lit by the moss. Only the ground was changing, somehow getting softer. Every now and then something cracked and crunched under our feet. Shining the light of my cell phone down, I noticed dark, small spirals with tiny bones and beetle shells scattered along the ground.

Before I had time to point it out to Anup and Pierce, we reached the next cave. Something was not quite right here. Sounds were muffled and I heard a low hum that seemed to come from all around us.

Just then, Pierce slipped right in front of me and nearly fell over, but he regained his balance before he fell.

"Yuck, what's that?" he yelled, jumping backwards a bit. Disgusted, he wiped the bottoms of his boots on a nearby rock.

Anup bent down, ground something with the tip of his foot, tilted his head up, and burst out laughing. "Bat droppings."

"What?" Pierce looked at at the ground with alarm. "Nuh-uh!"

"You almost landed in bat poop," Anup said. "But never mind, it could have been dog poop."

"Ugh, just great." Pierce reached for his canteen and splashed water on his boots. He stomped on in a huff, shaking his feet every few steps. The floor was covered with bits of bat dung.

"*Shush!*" Anup warned, pointing upwards. "Don't wake them, there must be hundreds of them."

Only now did Pierce and I follow his gaze. The roof seemed to be moving. Countless tiny dark bodies were swinging from it, headfirst.

"What now?" Pierce whispered in alarm and ducked his head.

"Now, we're going to find a way out of here," I whispered back. "And very quietly!"

We tiptoed across the room. All around us, the little critters were clinging to the ceiling and the rocky walls. We couldn't find an exit. Instead, we found the only bat-free spot, a rocky indentation low to the ground. We crawled in, ducked our heads, and looked at each other in despair. I picked at my T-shirt; I was starting to feel cold.

"Did we take a wrong turn somewhere?" asked Pierce.

Anup shook his head. "I don't think so." He opened his backpack and took out a lunch box with a lid. "Let's eat first and then we'll take another look."

Pierce snorted. "You think we'll see more on a full stomach?"

Anup's eyes narrowed sharply in warning. "I'm saying I'm hungry. You can either eat with me or keep wading through bat poop out there!" Pierce hesitated.

I couldn't suppress a grin. "I'd stay in here if I were you. No one brings food as delicious as Anup!" I enthusiastically grabbed one of the samosas from Anup's box and took a bite.

Pierce did not hesitate long before taking one of the vegetable-filled pastries as well.

His eyes widened. "Yum, that's delicious! Your mom is a really good cook."

"My dad made the samosas," Anup said proudly.

And again, Pierce put his foot in it. "Oh, really? Is he a chef at that new Indian restaurant?"

Anup got angry. "My dad's a *doctor*, but he can still cook!" he grumbled. "Why does everyone always assume that someone from India has to work in an Indian restaurant?"

"Or..." I licked a crumb from the corner of my mouth. "...that only women cook?"

Pierce stopped chewing. "I'm sorry," he mumbled. And after a pause: "That's the way it was with us. My mom always did the cooking."

Anup and I exchanged a look. Then, without another word, Anup handed Pierce another samosa. We'd both noticed how sad Pierce sounded. And that he was speaking in the past tense, as if his mother were no longer around. And we'd seen with our own eyes that a meal together for Pierce, his father, and his grandfather was a takeout pizza and a few cans of soda.

So where *was* Pierce's mother? I took heart and said, "My parents liked to cook together in the evenings. But Dad doesn't live with us anymore...." I shrugged and left the rest unsaid. Anup handed me another samosa.

Pierce turned to me. "Did he leave you all of a sudden, too?" he asked quietly.

I wrinkled my nose. "Not completely. He still lives nearby." I rubbed my arms. "Mom and Dad say it's 'complicated'...."

"You're freezing!" Pierce rummaged through his backpack and pulled out a hoodie. "Here, take this."

I was surprised but slipped into it gratefully. "That's really kind of–" I didn't quite get the "you" out because I was interrupted by a sudden rustling and flapping of wings.

As if an inaudible alarm clock had gone off somewhere, all the bats woke up at once. They fluttered around each other and left the cave through a narrow shaft in the ceiling. A warm evening light filtered through and painted a circle on the floor.

We jumped up and craned our necks to see.

"Too bad we can't get through there," Pierce said with a sigh. I nodded.

Anup waved us over and pointed to the underside of a ledge that had been completely covered by the little creatures earlier. "Do you see what I see?"

Embedded in the rock was one end of a shiny chain.

We pulled on it. A small silver chest, engraved with the symbol of a BAT, fell from a hollow above. Inside was a roll of paper held together by a tattered ribbon.

Eagerly, we unrolled it: a dark square was drawn on it, with just a few words written along the edge.

"OK!" I leaned over the paper. "Here we go! What is it about this time?"

Well, it's about bats – or rather, one bat. Follow the cutting and folding instructions carefully because every millimeter counts. And most importantly, be sure to cut out the teeth accurately, or ask an adult to help you. When you have the folded bat, look for this symbol in the book and the accompanying booklet: It will tell you which corner to position it on so that the bat's teeth point to the digits of the code you need to find the next page number. And that's where you go from here.

Don't forget to write the word in capital letters on page 9 of Lucia's Secret Book.

0 5 9

▲ ★ Y

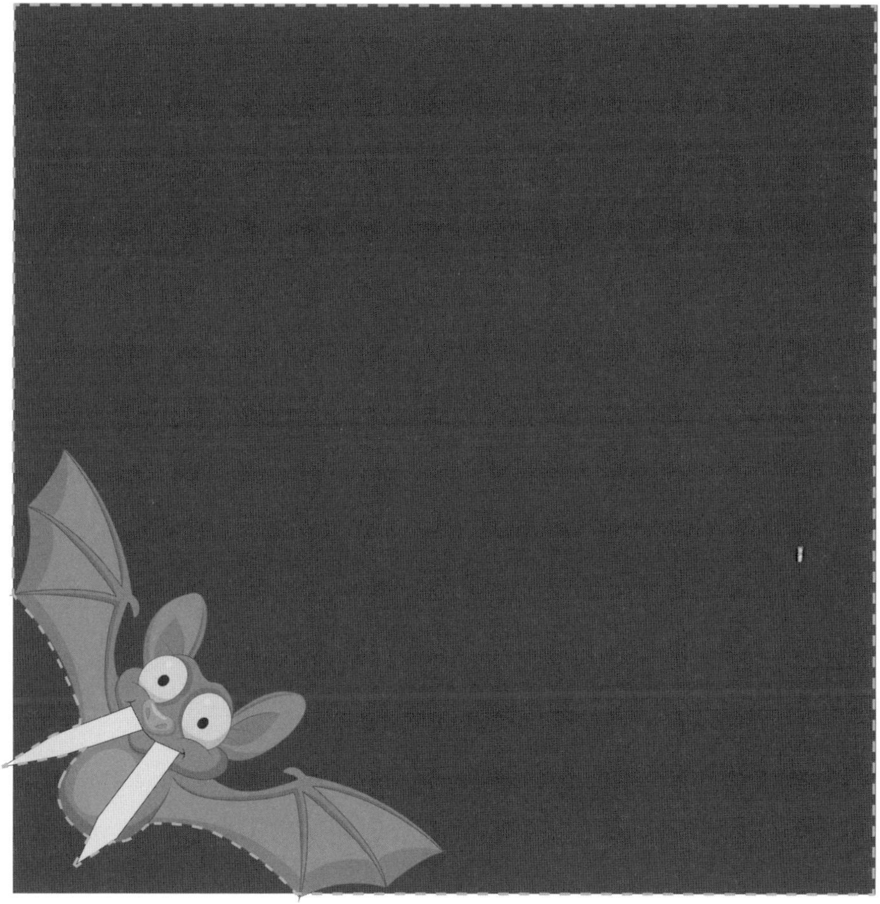

1. Cut out the square along the dotted line.

2. Flip the square over so the bat is facing downward.

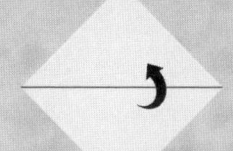
3. Fold the bottom half (where the bat is) upward, halfway along the square.

4. With your bat hanging upside down, flip the square so the bat is facing downward.

5. Fold the top corner down, bringing its top tip to the base of the bottom.

6. Now it looks like three triangles. Take the right side triangle and fold it over the center triangle.

7. Do the same with the left side triangle, creating a square.

8. Open the square up to the way it was before, with three triangles showing.

9. Tuck the right triangle's bottom right corner up and down behind the white triangle, like stuffing half of it into a pocket.

10. Now do the same with the left triangle's bottom left corner. This should create a diamond-like shape with the bat at the top, facing downward.

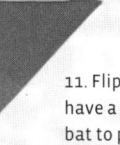
11. Flip it over. You should now have a nice little pocket behind the bat to put the corner of a page into!

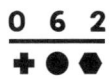

Was Anup right? Excited to find out, I ran up the hill on the other side of the lake. Would we really be able to see the rocks from there? And were they *the Three* that might be hiding the entrance to the Dragon's Cave? We had already passed some narrow shafts that led deep into the rocks, but they had been sealed with metal bars sometime in recent years. They looked like air shafts.

Behind me, I heard Anup stumble and slow down. It wasn't easy for him to keep up with my pace. Not only because I was pretty fast, but also because Anup's right leg was a little shorter than his left.

That was also the reason why he thought gym class was dumb. Except for swimming. He was brilliant at swimming. And diving, too! It was funny that his name – Anup – meant something like "close to the water." His mom had told me. In the summer, he would jump into any pond or lake, no matter how deep or cold. He just loved it.

I pretended that I was out of breath and needed a break so that Anup could catch up. Side by side, we reached the top of the hill. The trees there weren't as tall as the rest of the forest.

When my mom was little, even younger than I am now, there had been a prison here.

At that time, there was only a bare strip of land up here on the hills. The trees had been cut down so that no one could hide in them if they managed to escape from prison. But since then, the trees were left to grow, so the forest looked like a regular forest, only younger.

In the undergrowth, Anup and I discovered the remains of a watchtower. Its upper part and its door were missing, but the stairs were still there. Cautiously, we climbed up the steps to get a better view of the surroundings. As soon as we reached the top, we saw them: three rocks, not far from us, on the other side of the tower. They were all different sizes, standing close together, just as they were marked on my map.

The Three – we had found them!

Excited, Anup jumped from one leg to the other. "See that, Lucia? There they are!"

"At last!" I shouted and took his hand. "Come on! Somewhere over there is the entrance to the cave."

Together, we ran down the steps and down the slope.

Yeah, we had come to the right place, all right. The three rocks lay in front of us like the arrow-shaped tip of a dragon's tail.

We had just reached the first rock when we heard a rustling sound on the other side. Anup and I held our breath and listened carefully. The rustling stopped. But somewhere nearby, we could hear breathing or snorting. Who or what was that? A wild boar? Or was someone following us?

Anup pointed to the thick shrubbery beside us. We ducked into it as fast as we could. Behind the leaves, we were invisible to our pursuer. But what should we do now?

Anup put a finger to his lips and turned his head to the side of the rock that was hidden by overhanging branches.

I nodded. If we could get there unnoticed, we might be able to see behind the rock. I started to crawl forward and was about to take a peek when I heard another rustle. This time, it was much closer! I quickly ducked down and crouched on the pile of leaves behind me. At least, I *thought* it was a pile of leaves. A few seconds later, I knew better: I had parked my butt in the middle of an anthill! Yikes, they really knew how to bite!

"Ouch!" I yelped and jumped up.

I danced around, tugging at my pants and T-shirt, and stumbled out of the bushes. Anup came after me and brushed the red fire ants off my arms and legs.

Just two yards further on, we narrowly missed colliding with someone. Someone who looked very puzzled to see us: *Pierce*. Of all people!

Pierce was in our class at school. And Pierce didn't like us. And if Pierce didn't like you, you were in trouble. What Pierce believed or thought was the law, even though he didn't actually think for himself. Take the treasure in the Dragon's Cave, for example: his father claimed that the old legend was a fairytale for kindergarteners. And Pierce was convinced that his father was always right. He made fun of anyone who disagreed with him – and since Anup and I never really agreed with him, we both got the brunt of it.

But this time, Pierce stood facing us as if we had caught him in the act. He quickly hid a piece of paper behind his back. "What are you dummies doing here?" he asked. As if we had disturbed him in the middle of something important and not the other way around!

"We're looking for the entrance to the treasure cave. What about you, jerk?" I asked.

"Nothing!" Pierce stuffed the paper into his back pocket and covered it with his hand so we couldn't see what he was hiding. "Just walking around. Do you mind?"

I didn't believe a word he said. And I wasn't the only one.

"Yeah, sure," Anup scoffed. "That's why you brought a backpack. It must be empty since you're doing nothing, right?"

Pierce's lips curled into a thin line. He always made fun of others but didn't like it when people laughed at him. Then he'd get really mean. Like now. "The little weakling and the little witch!" His eyes darted up and down at us. "No wonder you two hide in the woods where no one has to look at you."

I quickly grabbed Anup's hand. He had grown a thick skin by now and had learned not to react when Pierce said something nasty to him. But if Pierce ever called me a witch, "carrot-top," or "ginger" because of my red hair... that's when Anup got *really* mad.

"Never mind," I whispered. "Who cares about that jerk?" But Anup pushed his chin up aggressively.

I pulled him back while Pierce continued to taunt him. "What's the matter, stumble-bum? Do you need a girl to protect you?"

"And you?" I shot back before Anup could reply. "Who is protecting *you*? I don't see any of *your* friends anywhere."

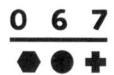

"True," Anup spoke only to me, as if Pierce wasn't even there. "He's not usually out all alone."

"Maybe there's a reason why today is different." I looked at Anup and grinned. "Maybe he's out with his grandpa's treasure map?"

Pierce winced. As much as he scoffed at the dragon legend, his grandfather believed in it, something Anup and I had discovered by chance a few days ago.

We had been asked to drop off Pierce's homework because he hadn't been to school.

"It's on your way, anyhow," our teacher had said. And that was that, although it wouldn't have been much of a detour for Pierce's dumb friends, either.

Pierce's home was very different from what I had imagined. In the overgrown driveway stood a broken-down car, with a car jack rusting away beside it. We had rung the doorbell, but no one had answered, so we walked around the house with its chipped paintwork. That's when we spotted Pierce's father through the window. He was sitting on the sofa with the lights out, his head buried in his hands. He was obviously too tired to open the door. He looked downright gray, like everything else in the room.

The wallpaper and furniture looked faded, as if all the color had been drained out.

The only thing of color on the otherwise bare wall was what looked like a map: a very *old* map in an artfully carved picture frame. I was about to press my nose against the window when Pierce's father had slowly risen to his feet. For a moment, I'd thought he had seen us, but he had shuffled off to the door.

Anup and I then quickly ran to the front of the house. Pierce, who still looked pretty groggy, had come back from shopping with his grandfather. Without a word, Pierce's dad took the pizza they had brought, pulled a can of soda out of the bags, and disappeared back into the dark house. Pierce had been anything but happy to see us. Only his grandpa gave us a friendly welcome. And when I couldn't contain my curiosity and asked if that was a real map on the wall, he didn't glare at me like Pierce, but said, "Yes!" and explained: "It might even be a treasure map. Or at least part of it." His eyes and the many wrinkles around them smiled. "If you want, I'll show it to you."

I had really wanted to see it, but before I could answer, Pierce interrupted. "They don't have time! And neither do we. Dad's waiting with the pizza." With that, he had pushed his grandfather into the house and slammed the door in our faces.

Now, here on the summer solstice, Pierce acted as if he didn't even know what we were talking about. "Treasure map? What nonsense!" He wrinkled his nose.

"Well, then," said Anup, "let's see what you have hidden in your pocket." Anup looked at the yellowed piece of paper sticking out of Pierce's back pocket.

Hastily, Pierce turned away and took a few steps back. "None of your business!" he growled so angrily that we probably wouldn't have dared to follow him.

But then he tripped over a root, stumbled... and was gone!

All we could hear was *"Aaargh! Help!!!"* followed by clattering and rumbling.

"What in the world was that?" Anup stared at the spot where Pierce had stood just seconds earlier. "Where did he go?"

"I don't know!" I was as shocked as he was.

Cautiously, we moved forward. Between the roots of the bushes, we discovered an old broken grate. Below it, a sloping shaft led a short way down into the mountain. At the bottom of it, Pierce shakily brushed some leaves and dirt from his hands.

"Did you hurt yourself?" I called down to him.

"Don't ask stupid questions!" he replied angrily. "Just get me out of here!"

Anup snorted. "It doesn't *seem* like he's hurt."

I took a closer look at the hole. "Do you think this could be the entrance to the Dragon's Cave?"

Anup shrugged his shoulders. "I don't know. It looks more like one of the air shafts we came past."

That was true. But where was the entrance? Maybe behind the third rock?

"Hey, what are you waiting for?" Pierce shouted impatiently. "Hurry up and *do* something!"

I took off my backpack. "Hey, Anup, if we get Pierce out of there..." I grinned, pulling out the rope. It was quite a bit longer than my mom's jump rope. "...then he owes us, right?"

"Hmm." Anup grabbed the rope and tied it around a nearby tree trunk. "You're right about that."

I slowly lowered the rope into the shaft before pulling it up again so that Pierce couldn't reach it. "What do you offer us in exchange for our help?" I asked innocently. "I think if we rescue you, you should owe us something."

Pierce was always giving Anup and me a hard time. This was our chance!

"Have you lost your mind?!" Pierce shouted from below. "It's your fault that I'm stuck down here!"

There he was at the bottom of the shaft, jumping furiously towards the end of the rope but with no chance of reaching it.

Gritting his teeth, he relented. "All right! You win, little witch!" Then he quickly corrected himself. "I mean, Lucia! Get me out of here, and I'll never call you a witch again. Or a ginger!"

I leaned further forward. "And you won't make fun of Anup's leg anymore?"

"Promise!" Pierce exclaimed.

Satisfied, I straightened up. Ha! For the first time ever, Pierce did what we said. For the first time, he promised to leave us alone. And all it had taken was him getting stuck in some old air shaft.

"Come on, let's get him out!" Anup gave me a little nudge. "He sounds like he's scared!"

Anup was like that. Anup didn't hold grudges. He had compassion for everyone, even for Pierce.

Still, I wouldn't want to be in Pierce's shoes, either, so I let the rope down a bit more. "Are you OK on your own?" I called down to Pierce.

Pierce looked at me with uncertainty. "What do you mean?"

"Well, can you climb this?" I pulled the rope taut and planted my legs firmly into the ground so I could hold it steady.

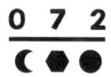

Without warning, Pierce grabbed the rope and jumped up, beginning to climb. The muscles in my arms burned, and Anup and I had to push backward with our entire body weight. "Whoa, he's heavy!" I gasped.

At least Pierce was hurrying up. With his legs braced against the rock face, he climbed up with impressive speed. He was vigorously reaching with one hand over the other again when suddenly there was a loud creaking sound. Anup and I barely had time to look over our shoulders before the rope snapped. Anup was thrown against me from behind. In front of me, I saw Pierce fall in slow motion. Then the walls of the shaft rushed past me. In panic, I let go of the rope and put my hands out in front of me. I was falling, down, down, down...

Continue reading on page 111.

I turned the corner and could not believe my eyes. I
had never seen anything like it before. Not even Pierce
could think of something to say. It was impossible to
tell exactly how big the cave was. Our light didn't even
reach into every corner, and there were spikey rock
formations everywhere, growing from the ceiling and the floor.
Some of them met in the middle and merged into glittering
columns. Others looked like icicles, their tips pointing either up
or down. These were called stalactites and stalagmites, as I had
learned on one of our family vacations. They were formed
when dripping water deposited tiny particles that had been
dissolved from the rock, and they could take several decades
to form. And there, before us, was a maze of them! They were
packed so tightly together that we had to carefully squeeze
between them. I wondered how on earth we were going to find
a way through them.

"Good thing you brought that string!" Pierce shuddered uneasily.

Anup nodded. "You could go around in circles forever and not
even notice."

I gulped. Now would be a good time to confess that
there was nothing left of the ball of string.

But Pierce continued, "This is trickier than the mirror
maze my parents took me to for my birthday.

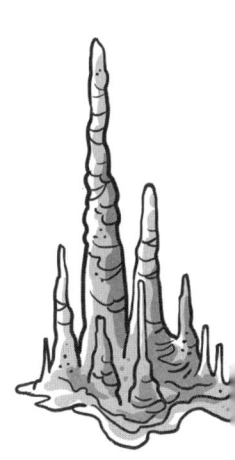

Before... " He stopped, digging his hands into his pockets. "Never mind. I mean, it's a good thing we have something to get us out of here if we go the wrong way."

"Yeah, well, I think I have something to confess." I tugged at my earlobes nervously. "The string ran out before we got to the cave lake."

It took a moment for the penny to drop.

"You left it behind?" Pierce sounded alarmed. I nodded.

Anup bit his lower lip. "So, we don't have a plan B if we get lost here?"

For the first time since we'd been in the cave, he looked reluctant to continue. I knew how he felt.

"I didn't know we'd end up in a maze," I defended myself. "I'd have totally saved the string if I had known."

"Never mind, we really needed it at the beginning," Pierce shrugged. "But maybe we're in luck." He bent down and looked at the clumps of dirt and debris on the ground. "Stalactites are made of limestone, right?" Confidently, he picked up a rock. "There you go! A limestone." I didn't get it.

Anup, on the other hand, knew immediately what Pierce meant. "Of course! Limestone is soft, a bit like chalk." He gave Pierce an impressed look. "Good thinking, Pierce. We can use it to trace our route back."

Pierce grinned proudly and drew an X at the base of the stalagmite next to him. When I ran my fingertips over it, it rubbed off. It did feel a bit like chalk. Yes, this could work.

"All right," Anup said. "Let's proceed logically: we'll start at the far left, and if that doesn't lead us anywhere, we'll take the passage right next to it. And so on until we get to the other side. Ready?"

Pierce held up the piece of limestone as a signal. He and Anup disappeared between two stalactites. I quickly followed them. A few turns later Anup stopped. "Dead end!" he shouted from the front. "We're turning around."

Now it was my turn to lead the way, using the Xs Pierce had drawn as a guide. I stopped between three stalagmites. "We turned right here!" I shouted. "But you can also go straight on."

I was about to set off when Pierce handed me the limestone. "The one in front is in charge of marking the way."

I squeezed between the stone pillars and drew an arrow on one of them. A few yards later I almost tripped over a baby stalagmite. It was too small for me to make a mark on it. There were several ways to go from here.

"What now?" I asked.

"Left!" Anup decided, taking the limestone from me and marking the intersection.

"How can you be so sure?" I wondered.

"I'm not!" he called over his shoulder and ran ahead. "I'm just thinking systematically."

"What?" Now I was *really* confused.

"He means we should always choose the same direction first," Pierce explained. "It's the best way to keep track when there are a lot of possible turns."

I scratched my head. "But won't we end up going in circles?"

He laughed. "Maybe, if we don't find the exit first. But if we do, it will be on purpose! And if we have to turn back, we will always take the passage to the right of the one we came from. That way we can be sure we haven't skipped any."

"That makes sense." I was surprised. I expected Anup to know this kind of stuff; he liked to read a lot. But Pierce? "How do *you* know that?" I asked.

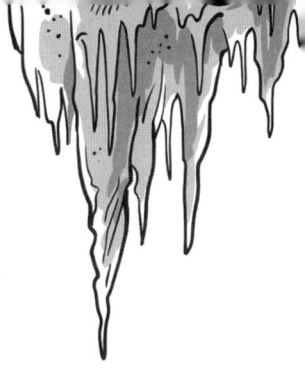

Pierce shrugged. "I like mazes. My parents and Grandpa used to take me on trips..." He trailed off and started again. "...before we stopped."

He sounded sad. I had never seen Pierce sad before. I gave him a searching sideways glance as Anup turned around. "This doesn't lead anywhere. We have to go back." He pressed the limestone into my hand. "Give it to Pierce and let's try the next passage."

Pierce led us back to the mini stalagmite, then took off into the next passage. I thought it looked like all the others. How were we ever going to get out of here?

"Lucia? Anup? I think I've found something!" Pierce sounded perplexed. An echo could be heard from somewhere.

Continue reading on page 041.

"Seven! It's the passage with the seven symbols!" Anup burst into excited laughter.

"The one that has the three siblings with the caravan of their peoples, the king, the sun, and the GEMSTONE!" I was so happy that I started bouncing up and down like a rubber ball.

"Great teamwork!" Not even Anup was able to stand still.

To my surprise, Pierce didn't respond with a silly remark, but instead patted us both on the shoulder, so hard that it almost knocked the wind out of me.

"*Oops*, sorry!" Pierce's ears turned red. "But Anup's right, isn't he? We did an awesome job – the three of us!"

We. The three of us. Just a few hours ago, Pierce would have bitten his tongue off rather than say something like that. But he seemed to mean it, so I didn't rub his nose in it. I waved happily to the siblings and the king above me. Then I ducked my head and started running down the passage.

It was dark and narrow. I was glad to have Anup and Pierce right behind me, not least because the ball of red string had shrunk quite a bit by now. Unless we were lucky, it would be gone before we reached the end of the passage.

But I would worry about that if it happened. For now, I was thankful that we were finally making progress.

The passage was getting narrower and narrower, the ceiling lower and lower. We were heading deeper into the mountain. Apart from Pierce's and Anup's footsteps, there was only one sound: dripping water. The farther we got, the louder it became. Even the air was getting damper.

An icy drop fell on the back of my neck. I winced and ran faster. This passage had to lead somewhere, right? Somewhere that wasn't so narrow and cold and wet.

I turned the next corner, then another. Nothing. Just darkness and rocks. I was beginning to find the blackness beyond our flashlight beams hard to deal with. I reached out and felt along the walls. They were so close! My throat tightened, but then I saw a faint glow of light ahead of me.

"I can see something!" The feeling that the tons of rock piled up above us were resting directly on my shoulders lifted.

Moments later, the cramped passage opened onto a narrow platform overlooking a huge cavern.

The ceiling above us was so high that we had to tilt our heads back to see it. Here and there it was dotted with air shafts, through which otherworldly, dim light fell on the wet, shiny rocks. Thank goodness we hadn't fallen through one of them earlier!

Below us, crystal clear water glittered, shimmering blue. It reflected the rock walls and, as we leaned closer, our astonished faces.

"A cave pond?" muttered Pierce, not sounding too happy.

"More like an underwater lake!" Anup's eyes lit up. "Let's have a closer look."

He had barely finished his sentence before he was running down the stone slabs that led to the bottom like a natural staircase. At the speed he was going, I was a little worried that Anup might slip. But the stones were wide and flat and I was glad I hadn't said anything. Anup really didn't like being treated like a baby. But who does?

When we reached the bottom, Anup pointed to the rock walls all around. "See that? When it's not as hot and dry as it is now, the water level is much higher."

Greenish-brown streaks covered the rocks mere inches above the water; they looked almost like moss, only more slippery. Anup knelt down, rubbed some of it between his thumb and forefinger, and sniffed it.

"These are algae," he explained. "They're underwater plants."

Pierce, who had taken a surprisingly long time to catch up with us, wrinkled his nose. "Algae? Yuck, it's slimy and gross!" He stayed as far away from the streaks and the water as possible. "And what do we do now? We can't exactly wait until the lake is completely dry and then wade to the other side, can we?"

"Hmm..." I inspected the cave walls. "We have to get across. It's where it all continues."

There was an archway on the exact opposite side of the lake. In front of it, the rocks formed a small ledge, like a balcony without a railing. It reached almost to the middle of the lake, as if nature had built a small bridge. Or rather, half a bridge.

Anup followed my gaze. "Too bad the boulder isn't two yards further out, or we could take a running start and jump across."

Doubtfully I tilted my head. It would still be quite a long jump, not to mention the uneven ground we'd be running on. Even I got the jitters just thinking about it.

"I don't know," Pierce chimed in. "Running and jumping aren't really your strong points. It would be easier if Lucia and I threw you over." He chuckled. I looked up angrily and was about to give Pierce a good scolding, when he continued. "If we had a rope, we could throw it over that broken peak over there and somehow shimmy across. You're really good at that."

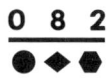

I really didn't get it at all. First Pierce insults Anup and then tells him how great he is? Anup didn't seem to know what to say, either.

Pierce raised his hands in apology. "Like the other day on the school trip," he explained quickly, "when we were all shimmying across the ropes in the adventure playground. Apart from me, you were the only one who made it to the other side."

He had noticed that? Maybe Pierce was not as big an idiot as I believed? I hadn't even finished that thought when Pierce ruined it. "I guess it's like poetic justice. Weak legs but strong arms."

Anup didn't waste any time. He pushed so close to Pierce that their noses almost touched. "I'll show you my strong arms in a minute! Just one little push and you'll be swimming to the other side."

"What? No!" Alarmed, Pierce jumped back so far that he hit the rocks behind him. "I didn't mean it like that!"

"Then what *did* you mean?" asked Anup.

Pierce hung his head. "Umm... I just meant, well, I thought..."

"You *thought*, did you?" Anup's eyes were dark with anger. "Thinking doesn't seem to be *your* strong point!"

Pierce shut his mouth and didn't say another word. But he looked glum, not at all his usual cocky self.

Anup left him standing and walked over to me. "The water may not be very deep now, but it's still freezing. So definitely no swimming or wading."

I nodded. "The bridge is much too high anyway. There's no way we could clamber up from the water. Not without a rope. Although," I set my backpack down, "I do have another one."

"If it's as tattered as the one before, it won't do us any good," Pierce chimed in from behind.

"It's not! It's actually brand new!" I shot back.

"*Is* it?" Pierce sounded angry. "Then why did you throw me the broken one? Maybe you did it on purpose?"

"Because the other one wasn't long enough!" I growled back. "You just *had* to fall into that deep shaft!"

"As if I planned it!" Pierce shouted angrily.

Anup raised both hands. "Cut it out, or we'll be stuck here forever! The passage we chose here was the right one. That means there must be some way across the lake. Maybe it's a secret again. We just have to find it, and it will be faster with the three of us. So please continue your fight on the other side."

"*Hmph*," I grumbled, but of course Anup was right: six eyes see more than four.

We were all scanning the rocks when we heard a soft splashing sound, followed by Pierce's voice: "Uh, guys?" His voice sounded shaky. "I think I just saw something moving through the water."

"What, a dragon?" I grinned.

"A dragon, a rat, an underwater monster, I don't care. But you couldn't make me so much as put a finger in there!" Pierce backed away from the water's edge as far as he could.

And when I looked down, I also swallowed hard. Circles of ripples were spreading across the previously calm surface, as if something had jumped in. Or, as if it had raised its head above the surface, spotted us, and ducked back under.

"Maybe a bat let one rip?" Anup giggled.

"Fine, go ahead and make fun of me," Pierce grumbled but didn't move an inch. "Bat farts, what nonsense!"

"Not at all, look up." Anup pointed to a boulder high above the lake.

There, we saw five misshapen, dark shadows hanging upside down. One of them swayed back and forth, then stretched out, unfolded its wings and wrapped them around its tiny body.

"When one of them had to go, it went 'plop' right into the water," Anup teased Pierce. "Just to make you jump."

"Bats?" Pierce raised his head. "But they're all hanging upside down! They'd just poop on their own heads!" He glared at Anup angrily. "You're talking total donkey doo-doo!"

"Donkey doo-doo?" I started to giggle and simply couldn't stop. "It's not donkey doo-doo! If anything, it's bat doo-doo!"

Anup looked at me for a moment, then snorted so hard that he choked. Even Pierce, who had fought hard to keep his composure, couldn't help himself. We laughed until our sides hurt and we had to sit down.

"That's..." Pierce gasped and wiped tears of laughter from his face. "This isn't funny at all!"

"No?" I grinned. "Then why are you laughing?"

"I don't know!" He tried to keep a straight face, but all it took was one look at Anup and me and we all started cracking up again.

"*Phew!*" I finally sighed, completely exhausted, and fell onto my back. As Pierce said, it wasn't the funniest joke, but it had come at just the right time.

"Too bad none of us can communicate with the bats," Anup chuckled, hiccuping from laughing. He held his breath and stretched out on the uncomfortable rock next to me. "Maybe they could give us a clue about how to get to the other side."

"Yes," Pierce agreed. "Anything has to be better than swimming. Especially if there's a load of bat poop in there." He became more serious. "Maybe we should turn around and try one of the other passages."

"What? No!" I sat up. "This is the way, I'm sure of it. You said it yourself: all three of us together cracked the riddle. That means we will all continue on this route together!"

"Um, Lucia?" Anup was still lying on his back with his head turned to the side. "I think I've made a discovery!" He held out his index finger.

At first, I couldn't see anything unusual, but then I saw a very faint, greenish glow.

"What on earth is that?" I jumped up as Pierce shone his flashlight along the side wall. There! Three circles, one on top of the other, gleaming in a plant-green color. The glow was mysterious, as if it came from within somehow.

"Are they spinning?" Pierce asked in surprise.

"Could be." Although... I really wasn't sure.

"I think it just looks like they are." Anup ruffled his hair, as he always did when he was thinking. "Maybe they're l uminous mosses?"

"Luminous mosses? What nonsense are you making up *now?*" Pierce scolded.

"I'm not making it up, they *do* exist!" Anup insisted. "When you shine a light on them, some of it is reflected back. And so, they look like they are glowing."

"I need to see this!" Even as I walked over, I noticed depressions in the green circles. There were hollows in the rock. And something in them was casting strange shadows. As if there was something underneath the green shimmering stuff growing on them. I stretched out my hand.

"Wait, Lucia!" Anup shouted nervously. "It could be dangerous!"

But I had already reached into one of the recesses. "It's not dangerous, it's three gear wheels!" I was already turning them. They had to be here for a good reason!

I turned them one way, then the other. Nothing. "Give me a hand!" I called over my shoulder to Anup and Pierce.

"Maybe they all need to be moved at the same time," Pierce wondered.

"Or one after the other in a certain order," Anup suggested.

My fingers were already sore from all the cranking. I rubbed my palms. There were marks in them. But where had they come from? I took a closer look at the stubborn gears. Each one had a metal number in the center: four, three, and seven.

"Ha!" I exclaimed. "There are numbers on them! And there's more all around, in the recesses, too! From zero to nine. I wonder if we need to turn the wheels to one of them?"

Anup nodded. "Like a safe? Hmm, that could be it."

"Exactly," I said. "Ten numbers each, on three gears, that makes, um..."

"Endless possibilities!" Pierce finished my sentence.

"Oof, my head is already spinning," I groaned. "How on earth are we going to figure this one out?"

"Spinning, that's the key word!" Anup had taken a few steps back and pointed to the moss growing in and all around the alcoves.

"Huh?" I didn't get it. Pierce looked just as confused as I was.

Anup looked back and forth between us. "You said earlier that the mossy circles seemed to be spinning. Maybe they're telling us which wheel to turn and in which direction?"

"What about the numbers on top?" Pierce asked, puzzled.

Anup chuckled to himself. "I think they tell us how far we have to turn it."

Do you see what Anup means? In Lucia's Secret Book, you'll find three green circles similar to the luminous moss. Look at them very carefully and concentrate on them. Then (as if by magic) you will discover the direction in which to turn the gears shown on the next page of this book.

Once you have figured this out, turn the pointer of the top gear by four positions in the right direction. Turn the middle one by three positions and the bottom one by seven...

Did you spot the word in capital letters in this chapter? You should know what to do with that by now.

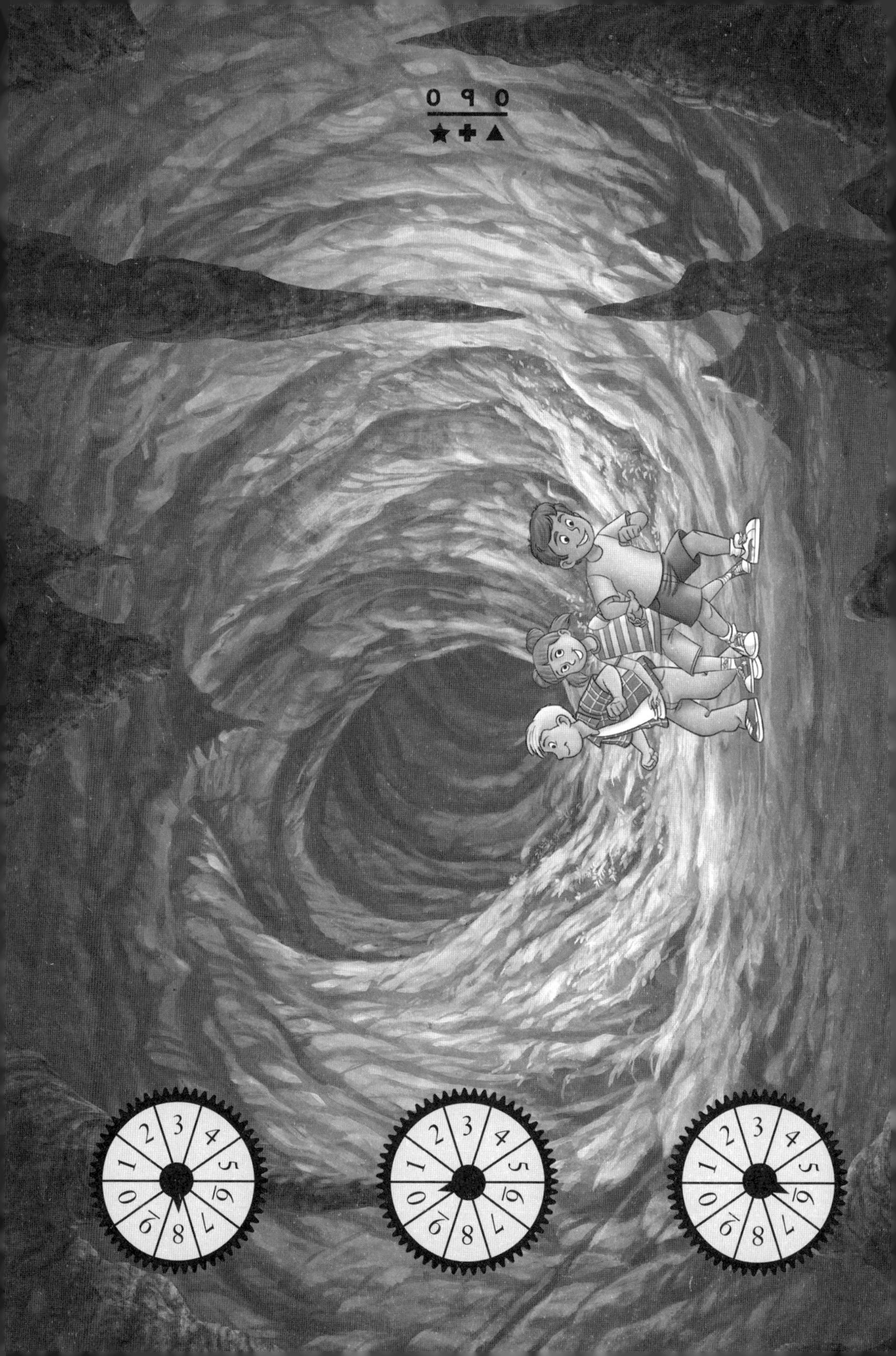
0 9 0
★✚▲
0 1 2 3 4 5 6 7 8 9
0 1 2 3 4 5 6 7 8 9
0 1 2 3 4 5 6 7 8 9

Even without dragons, getting down the tight path was difficult enough. Dim light streamed into the cave through a narrow shaft ahead of us. We could see a low passage next to a huge boulder. But it couldn't be the entrance or exit – the tunnel led in the wrong direction. I took the map out of my backpack, and Anup held the second part beside it. "Hmmm," he pondered.

Pierce grimaced. "Can you hurry up a bit? I want to get out of here."

For once, we had something in common: I couldn't wait to get rid of *him*, either!

"Well, I think we've pretty much been moving due west," I thought out loud.

"Due west?" Pierce snorted. "What are you? A human compass?"

I didn't answer him. There was no way I would tell him that I'd gone on the best adventure vacations ever with my parents. Back when it was still the three of us. I still had adventures with my dad when he and I went on trips together, but it just wasn't the same, even though he still taught me exciting things like how to find the points of the compass.

I pointed to the passage opposite us, which led upwards, unlike all the others that led downwards from the cave. "If I'm not mistaken, there's an exit somewhere up ahead!"

"At last!" Just like that, Pierce ran off without waiting for us.

Anup and I slowly followed once I had tied the red string around a rock – at least we would be able to find our way back if we took a wrong turn.

"Do *you* also want to go home right away?" I whispered to my friend.

He shrugged hesitantly. "Yes and no."

"Wait, what do you mean?" I asked. We had never been this close to the treasure! Today was the only day we could find it, and my best friend was going to give up before we even tried?

Anup gave me a nudge. "First, I want to know if we can get rid of Pierce."

I breathed a sigh of relief. It looked like Anup was thinking the same as me.

"Besides," he continued, "it would be good to know that we can get out of here if we want to. Wouldn't it?"

I shrugged at this and insisted, "We can also get out on the other side."

Anup tilted his head. "If what the legend says is true."

"Of *course* it's true!" I was completely sure of it.

Whoever found the treasure would also find a way out of the cave, just not the way they entered. Why, right there on the map you could see an exit and an entrance! But sometimes, I forgot that Anup was different from me when it came to this kind of thing. I always rushed in head over heels, while he always had to see the full picture first. That made us a good team. He always got into adventures and difficulties because of me. And because of him, we usually came out unscathed.

All right, so we'd find the entrance or exit first, get rid of Pierce, and then look for the treasure. It was a good plan.

Further ahead, we heard Pierce wailing, "Oh, no, this can't be! *No, no, no!*"

Anup and I started running towards him. As we rounded the next set of rocks, we saw what Pierce was so upset about: where there had once been an entrance, there was now just a huge pile of rocks and boulders. Only a small ray of sunlight shone through a crack at the top. No one could get through. Not even a mouse.

"Don't just stand there!" snapped Pierce. "Give me a hand!" He began to pull frantically at the rocks.

It took a while for Anup and me to convince Pierce that we couldn't dig through the pile of rocks. And it took even longer for him to quit pointing his cell phone at the narrow gap. I guess he was hoping that by some miracle, he would get a signal down here and his phone would work.

Defeated, he slumped down on the rock I was sitting on, studying our map sections.

"Are you done sulking?" I asked as I stood up. "If so, let's move on."

"Where to?" Pierce asked, picking himself back up.

I pointed back to the cave from which several passages branched off.

"Deeper into the mountain," Anup explained. "According to the legend, there's another exit on the other side."

"On the other side? Are you crazy?" Pierce hit the rock next to him angrily – and winced.

I could have told him that the rock was harder than his hand. Maybe he should have used his thick skull.

"As far as I'm concerned, you can sit here until you start growing moss and turn into a dragon," I said to him. "Anup and I are going now." I turned around and started to roll up the red string – we'd still need it. "Off to the treasure!"

Pierce jumped to his feet. "No way! I want a cut of that, too!" Typical Pierce. He didn't want to believe in the legend but wanted a share of the treasure.

"You're just like that dumb old king!" I growled.

"What king?" he asked.

"The one from the *legend!*" I couldn't believe it. Could he really have so little understanding? "He didn't want to believe in anything but wealth and power, either!"

Pierce grimaced. "*Should* I know him?"

"We talked about him in class!" Anup overtook Pierce and started walking beside me.

"In class?" Pierce repeated. "That wasn't class, that was story time! My dad says it's a complete waste of time for us to do legends and stuff like that in school. Real life isn't a fairytale!"

I'd had enough. "And my mother says there's a kernel of truth in every fairy tale."

Pierce laughed. "Your mother?"

I nodded and looked at him sternly. "Yes. And she knows, just like your grandpa. He kept a part of the treasure map and put it on the wall. Was that a waste of time, too?"

That settled it. Pierce shut his mouth and pressed his lips together.

And although I did not like it, I suddenly felt guilty.

I thought of his grandfather. Pierce probably liked his grandpa. Perhaps Pierce listened to him with fascination when he talked about the Dragon's Cave? And maybe Pierce just couldn't admit it because his dad didn't like it.

"Do you actually know anything about it?" I asked Pierce more calmly when we entered the cave again.

"Clearly not as much as *you* two professionals," he snapped back.

Well, it hadn't taken him long to start bickering again!

Anup nudged me, and I understood exactly what he meant: because the entrance was blocked, we were stuck with Pierce. We had better let him in on it. We still had a long way to go. We found the dragon symbol above the dark passage I had noticed earlier. There was absolutely nothing above the other passages, not even the tiniest lines. But the absence of a symbol could also be a sign. We would follow the dragon! Once again, I tied the red string to a ledge before we ventured further.

"Once upon a time," I began to recall the legend, "there were three tribes that lived here, led by three siblings: one tribe from the land of the lakes, the second from the small people of the mountains, and..."

"Siblings?" Pierce interrupted me. "What a goofy word. Why don't you just say three brothers?"

He was driving me crazy! It was just like him to think only in terms of boys.

Before I could reply, Anup explained: "Siblings are not always brothers. You have heard of 'sisters,' haven't you?"

I added curtly, "Is that so hard to understand?"

"OK, Princess," Pierce mumbled. "I just don't have any siblings..." He avoided looking at Anup and me. His ears were red as if he was embarrassed.

"Anup and I don't have any, either," I relented. "But we have each other: best friends." I gently poked Anup. He poked me back and grinned.

Hesitantly, Pierce looked back and forth between us. Then he nodded slowly. "OK, what about the three tribes and the... siblings?"

"Two brothers and a sister," I said, being specific. "The final sibling, the sister, came from the light-flooded plateaus high up. Together, the three tribes were infinitely rich."

Pierce thought he had figured it out. "And the treasure belongs to them?"

I shook my head from side to side. "They had riches, but above all, they were rich in happiness."

I waited for Pierce to make fun of it, but he remained silent.

"It was because of a magic amulet that each of the three siblings carried with them," I continued.

"*Magic?*" Pierce grinned. "Seriously?"

I nodded. "The king didn't believe in it at first, either. But he really wanted the treasures of the three tribes."

Pierce shrugged. "Of course he did. Anyone would. Did he have a nasty trick up his sleeve?"

Anup looked at him in surprise. "You know more than you let on, huh?"

Pierce's eyes widened. "What? No, that was just a guess... So, what happened then? Did he get away with it?"

"In a way, yes," I said mysteriously. "But not the way he'd hoped."

We came across some boulders in our path. I shined a light on them so Anup could see where he was stepping.

"Stop keeping me in suspense," Pierce pleaded.

Anup winked at me. He seemed to like the fact that Pierce wanted to know how the legend continued.

"He tried to drive a wedge between the siblings," Anup continued. "He wanted to make the brothers nobles in his royal court and marry the sister."

"But she didn't want to," I added.

"Why not?" Pierce was astonished. "It would have made her queen."

"*Pfff!*" I rolled my eyes. "He would have put a little crown on her head, but he would have been the ruler of the land that really belonged to her and her brothers. A great bargain."

"Yes, you're right, it doesn't sound too good." It seemed that Pierce was beginning to understand.

"They wanted to stay free," I explained. "She and her brothers. Freedom meant more to them than anything else."

"But the king was used to getting everything he wanted." Anup grinned at Pierce. "A bit like you."

Pierce took a deep breath, ready to object, but I quickly continued. "So the king got really angry and decided to take everything the three of them owned. But the siblings and all their people fled to the caves inside the mountains."

It was getting brighter ahead of us. Some light was spilling into the corridor from somewhere.

A few steps further on, we came to a circular, narrow rock chamber. There were five passageways leading off from it, and the ceiling rose high up as if in a spiral. There seemed to be narrow cracks through which some sunbeams found their way inside. These created bright spots on the walls where symbols had been etched. We looked around curiously.

"Is the amulet the treasure you're looking for?" Pierce wanted to know. He stepped into the middle of the chamber and looked up.

He didn't see me shrug.

"We don't know what the treasure is," I said. "But the story isn't over yet." I had his full attention again.

"Shortly after the three siblings and their tribes fled from the king into the mountain, he captured the youngest, who was the ruler of the waters. He had stayed behind to invoke the waters of the lakes and rivers to come to their aid."

"The waters?" Pierce swallowed hard and looked around nervously.

I nodded. "It was to prevent the king from following them, but he forced his captives to show him the way into the mountain."

"Oh, no!" Pierce said breathlessly. "So, if the king had the brother, he could blackmail the other two siblings into giving him whatever he wanted, right?"

Anup and I looked at each other. Considering that Pierce had insisted that the legend was child's play, he was now taking it quite seriously.

"Not quite," Anup reassured him. "He did have one brother and his part of the amulet, but not the others. And when he fled through the cave, the ruler of the mountains threw all the gems he possessed behind him."

Pierce grinned in approval. "A good distraction! I'm sure the king picked up the gems," he observed. "And the water kept coming in, huh?"

"Yes, the water kept rising and rising," I picked up the story again. "And the king had the gems, but he was still hot on the heels of the brothers and sisters. He had almost caught up with them, and so they abandoned all they had left: their pieces of the amulet."

I ran along the circular rock face. The symbols inscribed here were very similar to those we had seen earlier. I ran my index finger over the symbol of a sun.

"Just as the king bent down to pick up the pieces of the amulet..." I was nearing the incredible end of the legend. "...the sun appeared through a crack in the cave roof. Its rays connected all three parts of the amulet and led the siblings out of the mountain at the last possible moment. But the king who tried to grab the three pieces was blinded."

"And the floodwaters?" Pierce shuddered. "Did they reach the king?"

"Yeah, totally!" I took the Book of Legends out of my backpack and flipped it open. The end of the story was my favorite part. I guess because I felt that the greedy king got what he deserved. "The flood swept through the corridors and caves faster and faster. But the king paid no attention, trying to catch the pieces of the amulet that were floating off in all directions. Again and again, the king dived for them." I paused for a moment. "Hours turned into days, and days into weeks, and the king was transformed without even realizing it. His skin grew scales, his body became long and thin, and webs grew between his fingers and toes. Finally, one day, he had become a water dragon and no longer knew who he had once been. But he never forgot the treasure. And he still guards it to this day..."

Pierce gulped. "The king turned into a dragon?"

I shrugged. "That's what it says here." I held the book out to him.

"Yes, but..." Pierce looked cautiously over his shoulder as if he expected a dragon to appear at any moment. Then he shook himself and put both arms on his hips. "OK, you almost fooled me!"

"Fooled you?" I asked innocently. Admittedly, I didn't really believe that a human could turn into a dragon. Still, I liked the ending. "Well, I didn't make that story up. It's ancient. Just like the book. Isn't it, Anup?"

But Anup didn't answer. He was studying the patterns around the entrances. "Look, there are more symbols above the tunnels. Sometimes there are many and sometimes only a few. Like here: the dragon, a LEAF, and this one, but I'm not sure what it is..." He tapped on some lines that looked like flames.

"Maybe the symbol represents the ruler of the LIGHT!" I exclaimed excitedly.

"Yes!" Anup traced the furrows of another symbol he had discovered. "Then this could be a FISH. For the ruler of the waters!"

Now Pierce was enthusiastic as well. "And that one over there looks like a man! The king?"

Anup shook his head. "I think that's him here. See the crown and the SWORD next to it?"

Pierce wrinkled his nose. "True. The one in front of me is also much smaller. A dwarf, perhaps?"

"Yes, for the ruler of the mountains!" I held out my hand to Pierce for a high-five. "This can't be a coincidence!"

With a big grin, Pierce slapped my hand. "But what does the circle with the dot in the middle mean?" I looked closely at the symbol in front of us. "Hmm."

It was surrounded by three other symbols that reminded me of the siblings' amulets. And suddenly, I had an idea. "MAGIC!" I shouted. "That's what the symbol means!"

"Yes, that makes sense," said Pierce. "But which passage do we have to take? The one with the symbols of all three siblings above it?"

"Nice idea, but unfortunately, they're above several passages." Anup scratched his head. "The symbols surrounding them must mean something, as well. But what?"

Clueless, we looked around when I suddenly spotted another figure at the bottom of the wall. Could it be...? Sure enough, she was holding an open book in front of her! On the front was a circle with rays, just like the one embossed on the cover of the Book of Legends.

I held it up. "Anup, Pierce, look at this! What if we need the book to interpret the symbols and drawings?"

"Let's see the pages with the Dragon's Cave legend again!" Pierce asked anxiously.

With trembling fingers, I turned the pages. The old paper crackled as if it wanted to whisper something to us. And only now, in the dim light, did I notice that not all the words were printed the same way. Some seemed to be thicker and blacker! And they all had meanings carved into the walls.

"Of course!" Anup turned around in a circle. "The whole legend is depicted here, from beginning to end. Over there is the caravan of the three tribes going into the mountain!"

"And there's the dragon sitting on the treasure," Pierce added. Now I knew for sure: The Book of Legends would help us figure out which way to go!

Lucia is right. The legend on pages 2 and 3 of Lucia's Secret Book has some important clues for her and you about where to go next. To solve the riddle, find the words written in bold in the legend and connect them with lines. The next page tells you the order in which to do this.

Read the numbers from left to right and put them into your decoding strips. Don't forget to write the words in capital letters next to their corresponding symbols in Lucia's Secret Book.

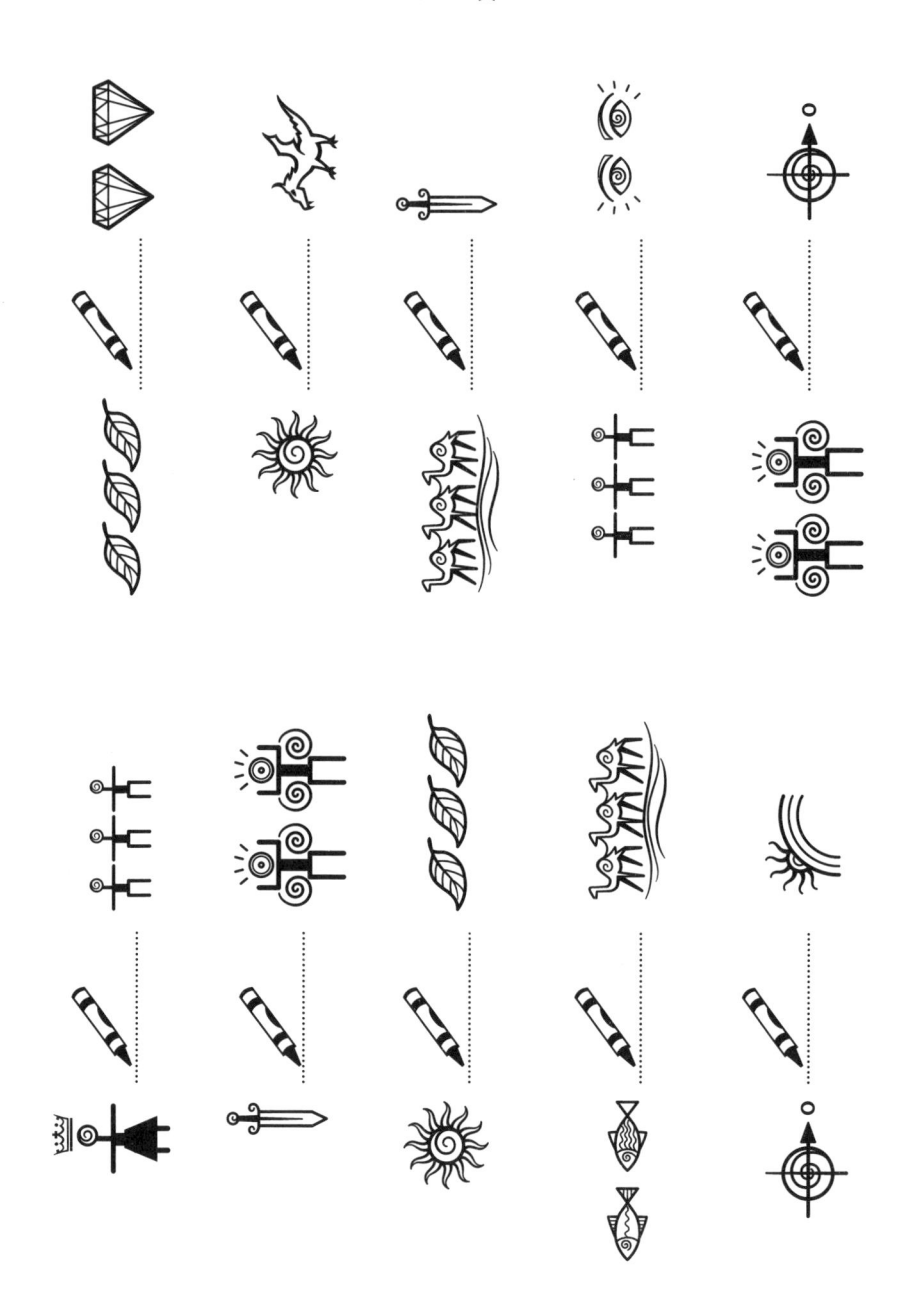

Pierce was kicking his legs almost faster than me and Anup. We had tied our empty plastic water bottles under his arms and around his stomach. Filled with air, they kept him afloat. Anup and I swam alongside him so that he could hold on to us if necessary. He was gasping for air frantically, but he kept paddling. He reached the waterfall first, held his breath, and, eyes closed, plunged through the splashing curtain of water. I stepped it up a gear. We came up the other side shoulder-to-shoulder, and Pierce hastily climbed onto the next rock. "Hurry up, you slowpokes." His teeth chattered. He smiled, held out his hands, and pulled us up. Shivering but happy, we passed through the heavy rock gate. Barely visible among the ferns and leaves, a staircase carved into the rock wound its way upwards.

We had barely reached the first step when a rumbling and crunching sound came from behind us. The gate closed tightly. No one standing in front of it would have guessed that there was a passage into the Dragon's Cave.

"So much for the idea of taking a shortcut," Anup sighed. I winked at him. "Don't worry, between the three of us we'll get through this maze of caves in no time."

We had just reached the top of the stairs and were standing on the edge of the cliff above the lake when the red sun disappeared behind the hills. Exhausted, we started heading for home.

We hadn't been on our way for long when we heard loud shouting. "Anup!" someone yelled. "Pierce?" called someone else, and then I recognized my mother's worried voice.

"Here!" we shouted back, as if with one voice. "We're here!"

Seconds later, my mom lifted me into the air and squeezed me so hard I could barely breathe. "I was worried sick," she whispered in my ear. "Why didn't you tell me what you were up to?"

"I didn't think it would *take* this long," I confessed remorsefully. "I'm sorry, Mom! And I'm sorry I stole the map, too. And the book."

"*Ugh*," she said, spinning me around. "I don't care about the map or the book. The main thing is that I've got *you* back!"

Next to me, Anup's parents took turns kissing him, threatening to ground him, hugging him, and asking if he was hungry. I couldn't help but grin.

Then I spotted Pierce's father and grandfather. His grandpa pulled Pierce into a tight embrace. Pierce's father joined them and hesitantly put his arms around them.

"What were you playing at, kiddo?" he whispered. "I was scared to death!"

Pierce shrugged, pulling his shoulders up to his ears. "You didn't need to be worried," he mumbled. "Anup and Lucia took care of me."

Pierce's father started to laugh. It sounded choppy and rough, almost like a half-sob. Or as if he had forgotten how to laugh. Then he pressed his forehead against Pierce's.

"It's good to know you have friends who have your back," he said. "But on your next field trip, you'll take Grandpa and me with you, OK?"

"If it's up to me, it doesn't have to be in a cave," Pierce's grandfather said.

"Huh." Pierce grinned. "How about a swimming pool instead?" He started to giggle. "We'll start in the shallow end, move on to deeper water with an instructor, and be out in the lake by the end of summer vacation!"

His father and grandfather shuddered as they looked at each other. Then they let out a collective sigh. "If it's absolutely necessary," Pierce's grandfather grumbled.

"I guess it's not a bad idea," Pierce's father said with a smile.

I laid my head on my mother's shoulder and took a deep breath. This time, Anup and I had not found the treasure of the Dragon's Cave, but maybe we had found something else, something much better? It wasn't just the two of us anymore. We'd become a trio, along with someone we hadn't expected: Pierce.

THE END

Congratulations! Turn to page 137 to find out how well you did in this book.

Fortunately, the shaft was sloped, so I didn't hit the ground completely out of control. But I was still shaken up. My right shoulder felt like it was on fire.

"Oh, no!" Anup shouted, sounding dangerously close.

I rolled to the side and bumped into Pierce, who jumped up frantically. With a thud and a groan, Anup crashed down next to me. The torn rope fell on us in neat loops, as if making fun of us.

Pierce rubbed his sore bottom. "Well, darn good job you guys did. Now all *three* of us are stuck in this stinking shaft! And we can't even use our cell phones down here! No signal."

Like it was *our* fault! I dragged myself to my feet, wiped my hands on my pant legs, and looked around. Pierce was right about one thing: without a rope tied to the top, we would never get up there. But I could see a passage behind him. The rock formed an arch, and I could make out some faint lines on it. Beyond that, there seemed to be more tunnels that I could only guess at in the dark. Was I the only one who understood what this meant?

I squeezed past Pierce, who was still grumbling to himself. Then I looked down the first rock passage, which also had lines and squiggles drawn above it. It was pitch black, and I couldn't even see the next turn.

I pulled my head back and took a closer look at the first arch. These weren't just lines. They were illustrations! They looked old, shimmering faintly in the twilight streaming through the shaft from above. I could make out a SUN, a CROWN, and, if I strained my eyes, even something like figures!

While Pierce continued to list reasons why this was all our fault and Anup argued against it, I shone my phone's light on the rocks behind the arch. I had also packed an actual flashlight, but unfortunately, the battery was dead. Luckily, Anup had also brought one with a brand new battery.

"We're not stuck anymore," I said, more bravely than I felt. "This is the way forward!"

Pierce and Anup stopped bickering and turned to me. I pointed to the passage on the left behind the arch. There was a sun symbol above it, another that reminded me of a TREE, and a third that looked like a big wave that maybe meant WATER. Then I looked at the other two tunnels. There were different drawings above each of them.

"Or maybe the way forward is over there," I guessed. "Or there, at that third passageway. And if we're lucky, one of them will lead directly to the treasure cave!"

"The treasure cave?" Pierce looked at me as if I wasn't quite right in the head.

"Of course," I replied. "We passed the first rock of *the Three*. If the shaft we fell down wasn't the actual entrance, it must be very close! All of this has to be part of the Dragon's Cave!" Determined, I unfolded and looked at the map I had borrowed from my mom. Darn. *Darn, darn, darn!* Disappointed, I dropped the paper. "It does show *the Three*, but... there's no indication of where we might be right now."

Though that was hardly surprising, was it? After all, I only had a part of the map. *Wait a minute!* "Maybe you can help us?" I turned to Pierce. "What's in your pocket? Your grandpa's map?"

Anup moved next to me. "It might actually lead us somewhere."

Pierce hesitated. And hesitated some more.

I leaned towards him. "Pierce! You just said it yourself: all three of us are stuck here. So if you have anything that can help us, let's have it."

"Don't you dare make fun of me!" he finally grumbled, pulling a yellowed piece of paper from his back pocket.

Small clumps of mud trickled to the ground. When he unfolded his map, it was full of brown-red streaks of dirt. Pierce must have traveled the entire way down here on his butt.

"No, *no!*" I exclaimed. "You ruined it!"

He turned around in a flash and carefully wiped it with his palms. "I didn't! Hands off!"

Seriously? First, he claimed that the dragon legend was nonsense, and now he wouldn't even let go of the map? He really *was* out of his mind! I pushed him and tried to grab it. Pierce gave me an angry shove with his shoulder.

"Don't fight," Anup cut in. "No one wants to take your map away from you, Pierce. But if it matches Lucia's, we might stand a chance of finding the exit."

"All right, then," Pierce nodded slowly. "We can hold them next to each other. But I'm not letting go of my half!"

And sure enough, the torn pages lined up perfectly. So, Pierce's grandfather was right. He *did* have part of a treasure map – the very part we needed!

All three of us bent over it, excited. But the initial joy soon faded. Although the two halves matched, they only marked the way to the entrance of the Dragon's Cave. As we could see on Pierce's map, it was still a good distance from *the Three*.

From there, the path twisted back towards the lake and ended at what looked like a stone gate. This had to be the high gate mentioned in the poem on my half of the map! Unfortunately, neither my map nor Pierce's showed anything about what it looked like underground and what route you had to take inside this maze of caves. And it really was a maze – not only the dragon legend said so, but the many different passages clearly showed it.

"Argh!" I handed my map to Anup, took off my backpack, and rummaged through it. Maybe I could find something to help us get back up the shaft?

"What?" asked Pierce, who obviously didn't understand what the problem was.

"The good thing," Anup explained, "is that we now know where the entrance is. The bad thing is that it's still a ways away." With his finger, he drew a line from *the Three* to the high gate. "I'm guessing about fifty yards as the crow flies?"

"Then we'll just go there," Pierce said. "If it's an entrance, it's also an exit, right?"

Was he kidding? Pierce really had no idea. "Fifty yards!" I said. "There could be endless twists and turns in those fifty yards. The Dragon's Cave is a maze! Everyone knows that! And we have no idea which of the three passages leads in the right direction from here!"

Pierce froze. "A maze?" he repeated, as if he hadn't heard me correctly.

I nodded. "Exactly. Dead ends, tunnels that lead nowhere, intersections. And if it were me who was hiding the treasure, there would be a few pitfalls, as well."

From my backpack, I took out the old Book of Legends that belonged to my mom and, to some extent, to me, that I had sneaked out this morning. I also took out the map and the jump rope. Next came the fishing hook and the red string I had collected on our way here.

The hook was useless, but we could use the line to mark the way if there were any intersections.

"Hmm," Pierce muttered. I was already curious what useless idea would come out of his mouth this time... "What about the back?"

"*What* back?" Confused, I looked up at him from my squatting position.

"The back of the maps, look! There's something there, too."

I glanced at the two halves Anup was still holding to the light. And because I could see them very clearly from below, I immediately understood what Pierce meant.

They were marked with lines, corners, and curves. But what did it mean? I jumped to my feet as Anup turned the parts of the map over and held them together again.

"It really looks like a maze," Pierce said.

Anup nodded. The routes were clearly visible. "The black boxes could be the shafts. In that case, we probably fell down... *here*. Or there." Anup tapped two spots along the edge of the map.

"Look!" I shouted. "Is that dirt, or is that an entrance and an exit?" I prodded the paper. And what I saw had nothing to do with the dirt Pierce's descent had left on the map. It was clearly a sign! "Let's go through the paper maze!" I said with newfound courage, pulling out one of the colored pencils that held my locks of hair together. "Maybe then we'll know which passage to take!"

Continue reading on the next page.

Can you find your way through the maze, too?
You will find Lucia's half of the map on page 119
and the other half in her Secret Book.

1. Cut out the map on page 119 along the dotted lines.
2. Put the two halves together and color in the route.
3. Can you see the three symbols? You will find a
number next to each symbol on page 5 of Lucia's
Secret Book.
4. Be sure to read to numbers in the same order that
the symbols appear from left to right in the maze!
5. Enter the numbers into your decoding strip.

Another important point: In this chapter you will
have noticed the words in CAPITAL LETTERS.
Go back and write them down; you will need them
for a later puzzle. There is space for them on page 7
of the Secret Book.

$$\frac{1\ 2\ 0}{\blacksquare\ \text{L}\ \blacksquare}$$

"Wild!" Pierce stared at the folded paper in my hands.

The drawing of the king had turned into a dragon. A large, triangular gem pointed to its left eye. Now we knew for sure which entrance to take: the left one.

Anup looked up hesitantly. "A leg up won't get us any further here."

I proudly pulled the jump rope out of my backpack.

"But this will!"

Pierce giggled. "Some kid's toy?"

I glared at him. "It's my mom's exercise jump rope. It's adjustable!"

Pierce held up his hands apologetically. "Don't bite my head off, Princess!"

I adjusted the rope to the longest possible length. Pierce took it and climbed onto the rock closest to the ledge above us. He grabbed one end and threw the rope like a lasso. The other end shot up into the air, flew over the ledge, and came down on the other side. Pierce reached out, caught it, and gave it a gentle tug.

"Nailed it." Satisfied, he grinned. "Who goes first?"

"Me," I decided. "Then Anup, and you last."

Uncertain, Pierce looked down into the dark water at our feet.

Then he took a deep breath and offered me one end of the rope, which came down to just above my head.

"Come on. Anup and I will hold on to the other end as a counterweight." He winked at Anup. "I mean, I'll hold on and Anup will hold on to me if necessary."

I stuck my tongue out at him, reached up and jumped to gain momentum. For a moment I swayed violently back and forth and almost kicked Pierce. Then I remembered something we had learned in gym class: I made a loop with my feet and stepped into it with one foot. From there, I pushed myself up and reached a few inches higher. After five or six repetitions, I breathlessly pulled myself up onto the ledge. Our gym teacher would be proud of me!

Still flat on my stomach, I waved to Anup. "Your turn!"

The jump was the hardest part for Anup. But he did it, then clamped the rope between his knees and pulled himself up using mostly his arm muscles.

A little later he was lying next to me. We both looked down at Pierce and I gasped. "You have no counterweight, Pierce! How are you going to get up here without the rope falling down?"

"Not a problem!" Pierce stood on his tiptoes and tied the ends of the rope together. Then he jumped up, hooked the back of his knees into it, took a few swings, and soon he was sitting on the rope like on a swing.

Very slowly he stood up and inched his way up hand over hand. He had almost reached us when he ran out of steam. "*Phew*," he gasped, "I need some help with this last part." Immediately, Anup and I grabbed him under his armpits and dragged him up to us. Breathless, we all collapsed to the floor.

"One thing's for sure," Anup groaned. "You may not be the tallest, but you're the heaviest of us all."

I giggled. "Maybe it's because of his big head."

"Excuse me? What are you trying to say?"

Pierce tried his best to look offended, but he was grinning. Maybe he wasn't such a creep, after all.

We ran along the passage without having to duck our heads, and we didn't have to make any turns. Luminous moss covered the walls like a pattern, reflecting the light of our flashlights in a greenish color. At last, we could see more than just a few steps ahead. But as we rounded the next corner, we stopped as if struck by lightning.

"And I thought we were finally getting somewhere," Pierce groaned.

Anup ruffled his hair, which was already sticking out in all directions. "This can't be happening, surely?"

Ahead of us, an ancient iron grate blocked the way. Its thick bars were embedded in the rock. Pieces of rust flaked off when we shook them, but they didn't budge an inch.

"Force isn't going to get us anywhere." Anup looked around.

"No," I agreed. "The three siblings of the legend didn't like the use of force."

"But they liked riddles!" exclaimed Pierce. "There must be a clue hidden here about how to get to the other side." While he and Anup started tapping on the rocks, I inspected the glowing moss. It ran over the rocks in winding lines and loops and turned angular right in front of the grate. Six-sided, to be exact. This couldn't be a coincidence.

"Guys?" I waved to Pierce and Anup. "I think the moss mainly grows in hollows in the rocks. And here," I looked at the wall in front of the grid, "it's stuck to some hexagonal stones."

Pierce glanced over my shoulder. "There are symbols carved into the stones!"

"Sun, water, tree, gem, man, crown, PAWS, and dragon." Anup was tapping the symbols as the stone fell towards him. "Oh, they're loose!"

"Maybe that's intentional?" Pierce pointed to the floor at his feet.

"And they belong here, don't you think?"

Baffled, we pointed our lights at the ground. We were standing on a polished stone slab with six recesses. They were arranged in a circle and each had six corners.

"Maybe some kind of board game?" Pierce wondered.

"You mean like Chutes and Ladders?" Anup asked. I was thinking more along the lines of dominoes and the jigsaw puzzles we had in the cupboard. Suddenly I had an idea!

Can you come up with an idea, too? Look for the hexagonal pieces in Lucia's Secret Book and cut them out. These are your game pieces. The stone slab shown on the next page of this book is like the board that goes with these pieces. Just like dominoes, the pieces must be arranged so that all symbols that are placed next to each other are identical. You may have to experiment a bit to find the right order for all the pieces.

There is only one correct solution. Once you find it, the arrows will show you the order in which to read the symbols to figure out the three-digit code. Remember to write the word in capital letters in Lucia's Secret Book.

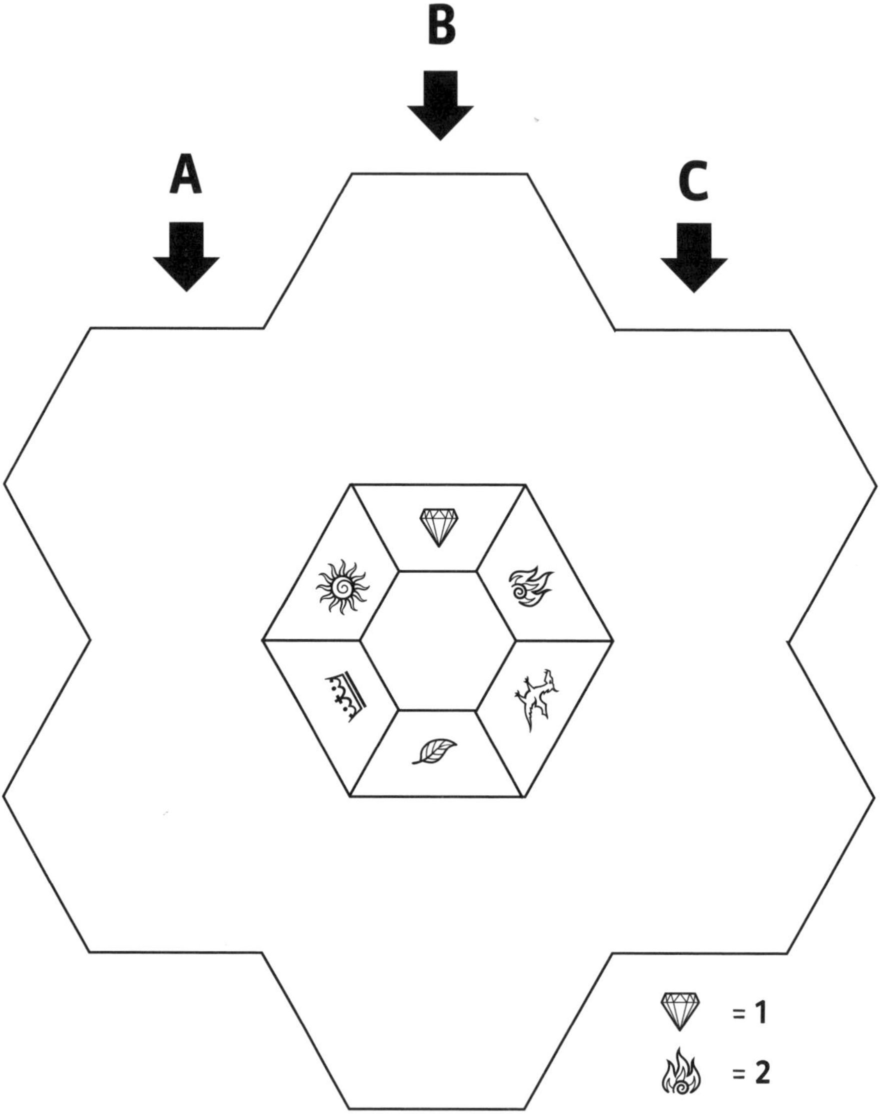
A
B
C

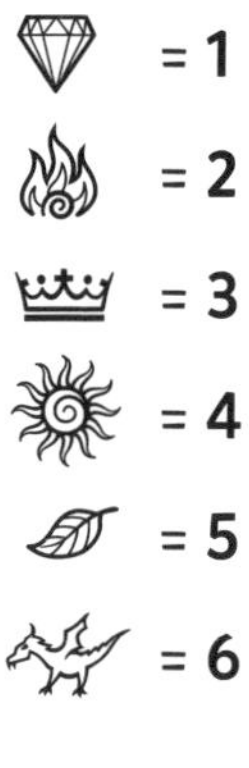
= 1
= 2
= 3
= 4
= 5
= 6

Phew! That puzzle was really tricky! For a long time, we couldn't agree on which numbers to set the gears to. But now they locked into place with a loud click, there was a clatter, and then a loud crack echoed through the cave. Something detached itself from a ledge high above us and rocketed along an old, rusty chain to just above the surface of the water, where it came to a swaying halt: it was a raft made of logs!

"How cool is this?!" I exclaimed enthusiastically.

Anup gave me a high five. But Pierce stood frozen, leaning against the rock face. "You mean we are going to paddle across the water on this thing?" His voice rasped. "That's just great!" He looked longingly back into the narrow tunnel we had come from.

"Give me a break!" I slapped my hands on my hips. "You're not going to turn around *now*, are you? We're on the right track!"

"Exactly!" Anup tugged at the raft.

The chain, which was attached above us, had gotten caught somewhere and gave way. The raft splashed down on the surface of the water. With a rattle, a few yards of chain followed, which would hopefully give us enough leeway to get to the bridge.

"This is proof that we have to get to the other side!" Anup had pulled the raft towards us by the chain and bent down to release a long stick that was tied to its side. "Or is the Great Pierce afraid of water?"

"What, me? Nonsense!" Pierce ran over to Anup and grabbed the chain so that Anup could climb onto the raft.

Carefully putting one foot in front of the other so he wouldn't lose his balance, Anup reached the raft and held out his hand to me.

I hesitated. Not because I was afraid, or anything like that. Somehow, I didn't want Pierce to be the last one on the raft. Maybe it was because of his posture. His whole body was leaning away from the raft and the water.

I quickly took the chain from his cold hands. "You first," I ordered, not giving him time to argue. Anup shifted his weight and held out his hand to Pierce. "Come on, then."

Cautiously and looking pale, Pierce climbed onto the wobbly raft. Anup had also noticed that Pierce was afraid. But unlike Pierce, Anup didn't make fun of him, instead trying to help him. Of course, Pierce didn't even notice, but that's why Anup was my best friend and not Pierce! I climbed in after him, holding the chain in my hand. Anup steered us across the cave lake with the long stick while I made sure the chain didn't get tangled.

A short time later we reached the middle of the lake at the half bridge. Only now did we see that it was carved on the right side. Narrow steps led to the top. Unfortunately, the first step was quite a bit above us, probably because of the low water level. Under normal circumstances, the raft would have docked further up. I was about to take off my backpack to pull out the skipping rope when Pierce launched himself into the air. Anup and I quickly stepped into the middle of the logs to keep the raft from tipping over. The buffoon could have warned us!

"Man, I'm sorry!" Pierce cried sheepishly as he landed safely. "I wasn't thinking."

Here we go again, I thought. But then Pierce reached out his hand to Anup. "You shouldn't be the last one to climb," he said, pulling Anup up beside him.

I pushed the raft under the ledge above me. Then I reached for the first step, but Anup and Pierce grabbed me, and before I knew it, I was standing next to them on the steps.

As soon as we reached the rock gate on the other side of the bridge, we heard a rattling sound that grew louder and louder. The mechanism was reeling in the raft's chain yard by yard. As if by magic, it was pulled back into its original hiding place.

"Wow!" Anup marveled. "What an ingenious system!"

Pierce, on the other hand, looked as if he had eaten something bad. "So much for the possibility of turning back!"

"Who wants to turn back?" Anup said, disappearing into the next corridor. "You've got to see this!" he shouted seconds later. "This is amazing!"

Continue reading on page 073.

With bated breath, we followed the instructions on the sheet and soon Anup was holding a small, folded paper bat.

"Wow," he said proudly. "Just like origami."

Pierce shook his head. "What in the world is *that*, now? And how do you know all this?"

I had to laugh. "Anup has the coolest hobbies. Anything to do with animals or plants, for example. And then this." I pointed at the bat.

"Folding paper animals?" Pierce made a face like he'd never heard of that.

"Not just animals, you can fold almost anything," Anup murmured, his ears turning red. "Robots, spaceships, really good airplanes and stuff." He seemed embarrassed that Pierce, the ace athlete, had found out that he liked to make things.

But Pierce was amazed. "Awesome! Could you show me how?"

"Um, yeah." Anup blinked in surprise. "Sure."

In the meantime, I had taken a closer look at the little chest. On the inside of the lid, I found some rhyming lines about the paper animal's teeth. They were supposed to point out the right way if you held them up to the sun. Most of the light came through the hole in the ceiling where the animals had escaped earlier, so I took the bat from Anup's hand and stood in the center of the circle that the evening light cast on the ground below.

I lifted up the bat. Its slightly crooked teeth pointed to the left and right of my feet. But there was nothing there but bat droppings.

"Wrong!" I lowered my arms.

"Maybe it should be upside down, like this," Pierce suggested, turning the bat in my hand upside down. "That's how the critters like to hang."

I raised my arm again, squinted one eye, and sure enough, one of the teeth was now pointing at the ledge we had just eaten under. I burst out laughing. "Looks like we got pretty close to the solution."

I bent down under the outcrop. Since the bats were no longer hanging from the ceiling of the cave, the sun's rays were shining down into the far recesses. What we had thought was the back wall of the ledge was actually two boulders. One stood slightly in front of the other, hiding the opening between them.

"Great teamwork!" I grinned, taking off my backpack and ducking into the narrow passage. "Follow me!"

We made slow progress. The tunnel got lower and lower, and I finally had to get down on all fours. I could hear Anup and Pierce cursing behind me. With great effort I pushed my backpack in front of me. Hopefully this wasn't a dead end!

It was so narrow now that we couldn't even turn around. We'd have to crawl backwards. Especially Pierce, who was a bit bigger than Anup and me, would have problems with that. I paused. Could it be that I was worried about him?

A rush of air hit me and the passage in front of me widened until it looked like a small vault. "Anup, Pierce, you've almost made it!" I yelled, standing up and looking around.

The room wasn't much bigger than my mom's workshop, but it was much higher. Five passageways branched off from it.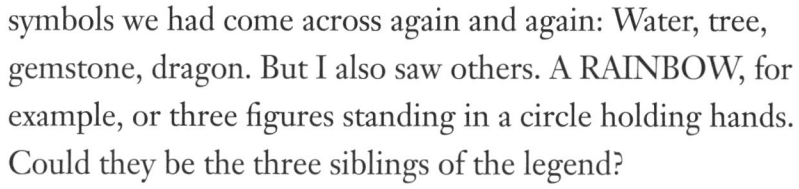

The walls between them were covered in drawings. I recognized all the symbols we had come across again and again: Water, tree, gemstone, dragon. But I also saw others. A RAINBOW, for example, or three figures standing in a circle holding hands. Could they be the three siblings of the legend?

Behind me, Anup crawled out of the tunnel and jumped up, shaking out his arms and legs.

Pierce emerged a few moments later. "Oh, man," he sighed. "I feel like one of your origami pieces, Anup!" He straightened and stretched, then paused. "I wonder how long it took them to draw all those pictures on the wall?" he marveled. "Some of them are really tiny."

"I'd rather know where we're supposed to go next." I pointed to the corridors that branched off.

"I'm sure we'll have to decipher the drawings to find out," Pierce guessed, and Anup and I grinned at each other.

It was crystal clear to us that the wall paintings contained a riddle. A few hours ago, Pierce would have made fun of it. Now he seemed to think along the same lines as we did. He no longer considered the dragon legend a fairytale.

I nodded at Pierce. "The drawings all have to do with the siblings. You see them? They're in a circle, holding hands."

"And over there, that's just one of them!" exclaimed Pierce. "The ruler of the mountains." Sure enough, there was a figure and a MOUNTAIN that looked like a jagged triangle.

Anup ran to the other side. "And here," he said with a smile, "is the ruler of the waters."

Thinking, I turned on my axis. "But where is their sister?" I wondered. "Where is the ruler of the light? Can you see her?"

Anup and Pierce's eyes darted back and forth. "You're right," Pierce said, puzzled. "The sister is only in this drawing of the three of them. She's missing in all of the others!"

"That must mean something." Anup flicked his flashlight over the nearest wall. "We have to look for her!"

Pierce stepped up beside him and pulled the limestone out of his pocket. "Let's walk along the walls," he suggested. "And I'll cross out all the symbols that have nothing to do with her."

He was already busy drawing a pale X over a dragon and a tree, the water symbol in the shape of a big wave, and two paws.

Anup beamed. "Fantastic idea, Pierce!"

I also had to admit that this really made things easier for us. And our limestone marks would fade away by themselves in time, leaving the drawings as they were.

On the next page you will find a grid of letters surrounded by various symbols. Check page 7 of Lucia's Secret Book to see what these symbols mean, and then cross them out in the letter grid. Now have a look at the remaining letters. Do you notice anything?

Remember to record any words that are written in capital letters.

L	E	A	F	T	G	E	M	S	T	O	N	E	H
R	D	R	A	G	O	N	S	W	O	R	D	E	T
M	E	E	F	I	S	H	I	M	A	G	I	C	R
A	R	A	I	N	B	O	W	L	I	G	H	T	E
N	G	B	A	T	H	W	A	T	E	R	T	S	E
M	O	U	N	T	A	I	N	I	P	A	W	S	X

$$\frac{1\ 3\ 7}{\text{☾▲★}}$$

How many clues did you use? Count how many boxes you checked on pages 11, 12, and 13 at the back of the book.

0   You are a total riddle genius. Incredible performance! Congratulations!

1–3   You've done remarkably well and should be proud of yourself!

4–8   Wow! You're really good at this! A very respectable result!

9–13   What a clever sleuth you are!

14–18   Not bad at all. There's every reason to feel good about yourself.

19–22   OK, not the best result – but not the worst, either.

23–27   We're sure you can do better, and with less help than you may think.

28–30   Don't be disappointed. There's always next time.

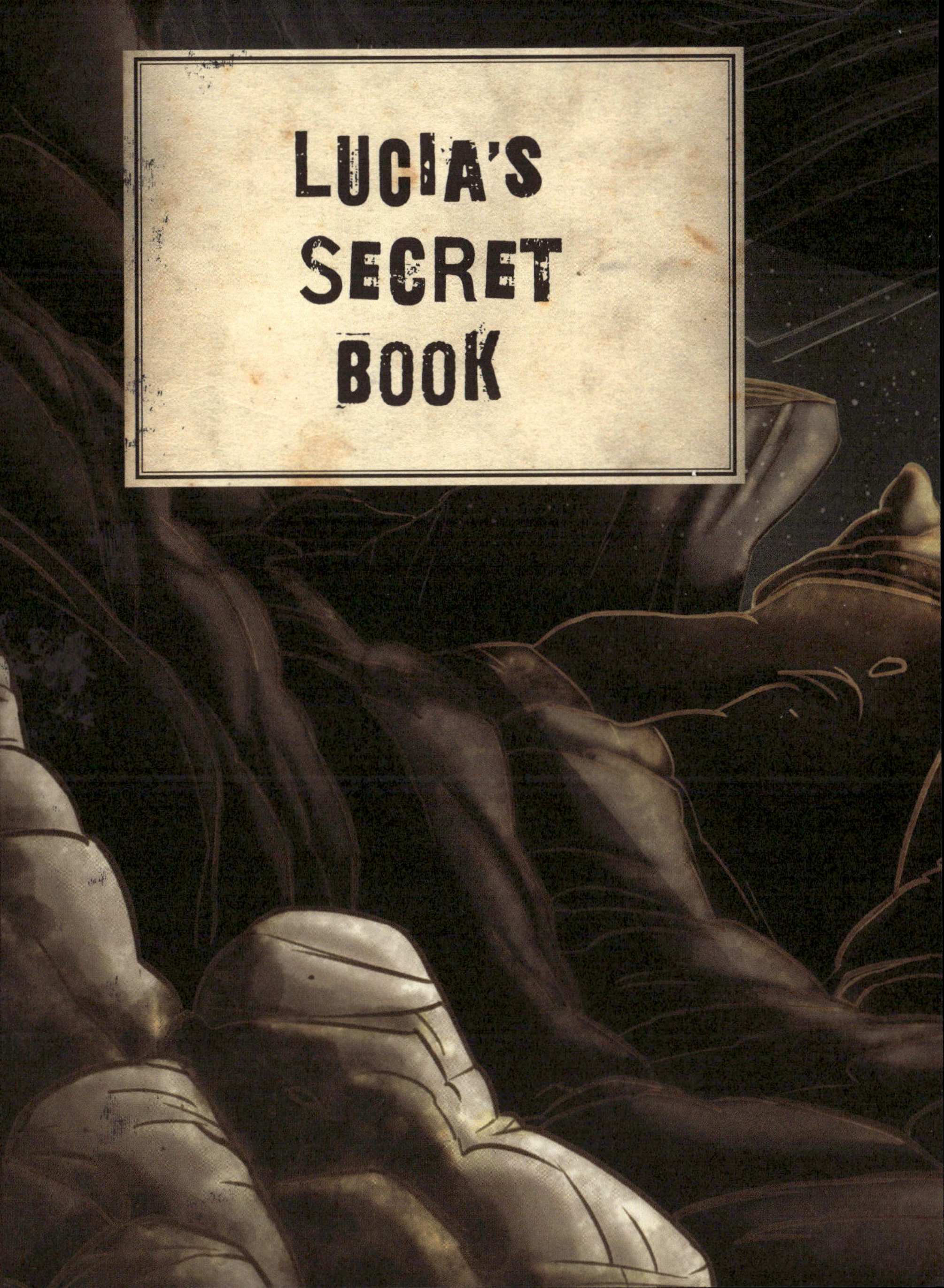
LUCIA'S SECRET BOOK

Once upon a time, there were three tribes living peacefully together. They were led by three sibling **children**: one brother hailed from the land of the lakes, where **fish** were plentiful. The second brother was from the small tribe of the mountains, where silver veins ran deep. And there was also one sister from the light-flooded plateaus of the heavenly lands. They all shared wealth, power, and good fortune, for they possessed a magical amulet of three parts, set with three gemstones. Each sibling wore one of these precious pieces, and their combined power was immense.

The king of the lowlands coveted all of this for himself. He did not believe in magic nor that the three siblings were powerful witches and great **wizards**. But he believed in their treasures, and so he did everything he could to divide the siblings.

He offered to make the brothers rulers over large estates with vast stockpiles of wealth if they would betray each other. The sister, he hoped, would be his wife and thus **queen** over all the land from north to south and from west to **east**.

But the siblings wished for another thing for themselves and their people: to remain free. This so enraged the king that he vowed to take everything from them: the sunlit plateaus, the mountains, the lakes, and most of all, the three-part amulet that was the source of their power. And so, he led his men into battle against the siblings.

The three took their tribes and fled into the mountains, into the secret caves that lay within. But the king was able to follow their footsteps' traces. The youngest brother, who ruled the rivers and lakes, had remained outside beyond the caves. He summoned the waters to gush forth from all around and hide the entrance from the watchful **eyes** of their pursuers.

The king seized the guardian of the waters, took possession of his amulet, and forced him to reveal the way to his siblings.

The king and his guards were soon drawing perilously close, for the **caravan** of tribes made slow progress in the darkness of the narrow passages.

In each cave they traversed, the ruler of the mountains threw gems into the hollows behind him as the floodwaters rushed in. The king always stopped to collect them greedily. Nevertheless, he caught up with the fleeing people.

With nothing else left, the ruler of the mountains cast his piece of the amulet into the water.

Sword in hand, the king bent down to grab the treasure. Hastily, the guardian of the heavenly lands caught the light of the **sun** shining through a crack in the roof with her amulet piece. As she dropped it, the dazzling beam found its way to the gems within the other two pieces. Blinded, the king and his men retreated.

Like a **rainbow**, the amulet's light curved to guide the fleeing people out. With all his strength, the youngest brother broke free of the guards, the last to slip through the secret rock gate before it closed. The flood swept through the corridors faster and faster. The king paid no attention to the warning voices of his men as they fled the cave. He tried to gather the amulet pieces, but they drifted away like **leaves** in the fall.

The king plunged into the flood, which swept all the **gemstones** from his pouches. No matter how long he dived for them, he could not reach them. Hours turned into days, and days into weeks, and the king was transformed without even knowing it: his skin grew scales, and webs formed between his fingers and toes; his body became long and slender like that of a serpent. Until one day, he had taken the form of a water **dragon** and forgotten who he had once been. Except for the treasure, which he never forgot.

And so, to this day, he continues to guard it.

Put the two halves of the map together along this edge. Start coloring in at the arrow that shows you the entrance to the maze.

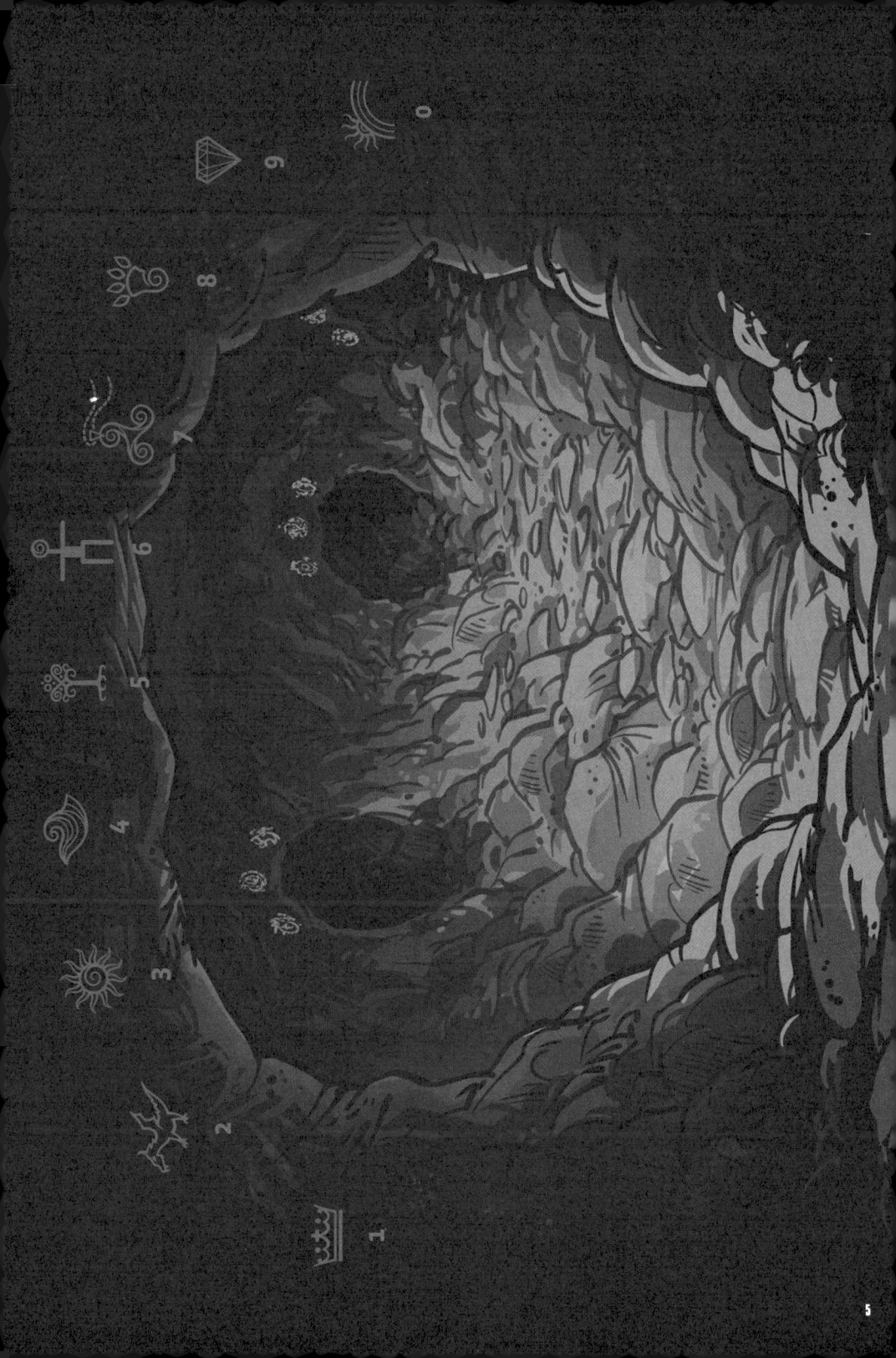

CAVE PAINTINGS

What do these symbols mean?

1. First, place the amulet on the image so that all the cut-out shapes show some of the color RED.
2. Then, place the amulet on the image so that only the two colors LIGHT BLUE and DARK BLUE are visible in one of the shapes.
3. Finally, place the amulet on the image so that no LIGHT GREEN is visible anywhere.

If you followed the instructions correctly, you now have the code!

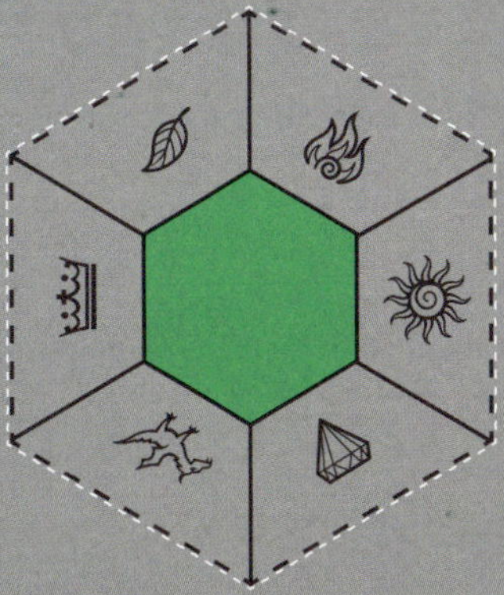
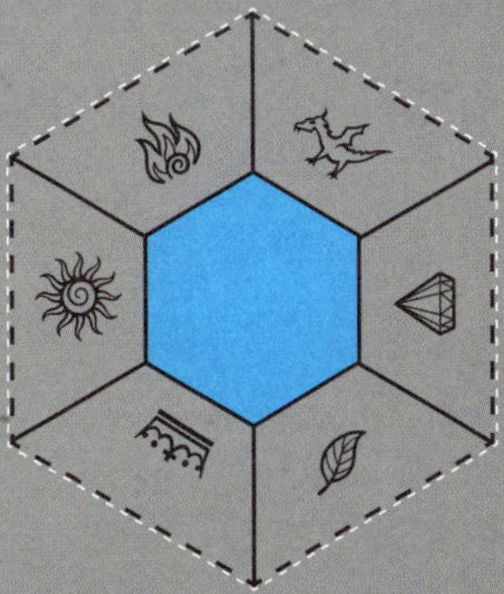
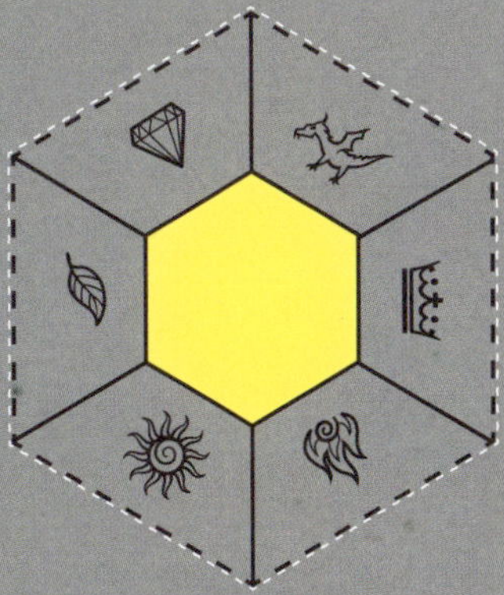
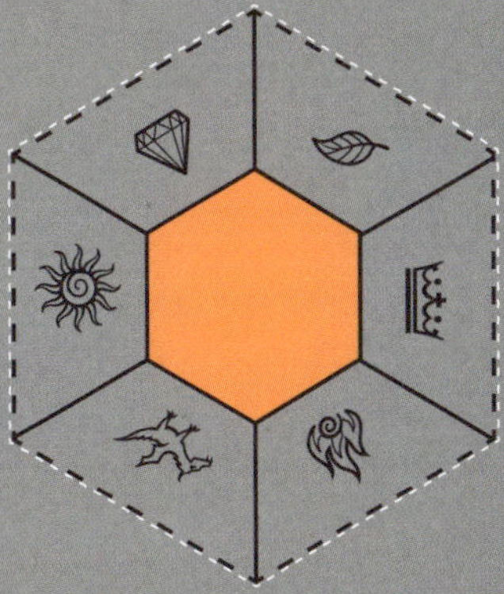
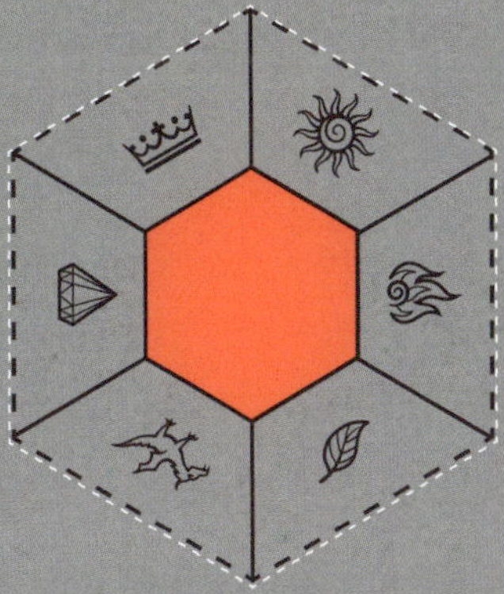
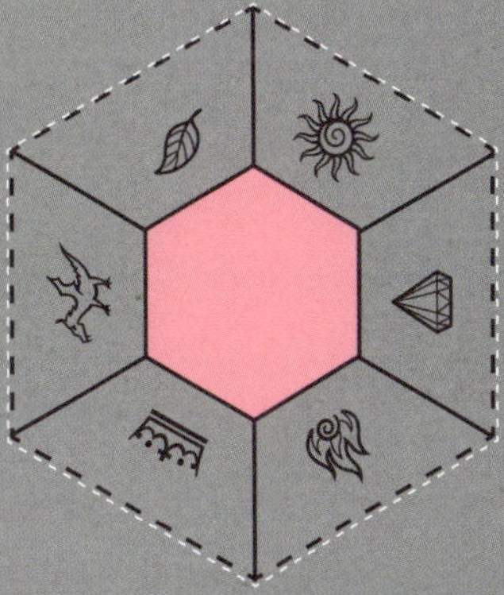

CLUES AND ANSWERS

There are three clues for each riddle. The page number of the riddle is given at the end of each line. If you're stuck, find the page number of the riddle you were working on last, and take a look at the left-hand star for that page.

Place the red plastic film (which you can find on the back cover flap) over the clue's text. And now, as simple as 1, 2, 3, you can read the clue. Should you need a second clue, do the same with the middle star. The right-hand star has the answer. Be sure to check off each box so you know how many stars you've used.

Clue 1
Cut out the illustration on page ??? along the dotted lines. The puzzle begins where it says "Start here". Follow the instructions and fold the page along the marked "?". Be sure to follow the new instructions carefully as they appear. Each time you are asked to count the gemstones, simply count the matching ones you can see and cross out all the others. Anything you can't see doesn't count!

Clue 2
Also follow steps 1, 2, and 4, and make sure you read everything carefully as it appears. You may want to write down how many matching gems you counted after each of these steps. This should make it quite easy for you to find the three numbers for the code.

Answer
After step 1, you can count 3 large gemstones, after step 2, you can count 7 large round and rectangular gemstones. After step 3, you can count a large rectangular gemstone but the code 371 in the decoding strips and it will take you to page ???

Clue 1
Take a closer look at the inside of the back flap of the book. You will see many colored gems on the back of the flaps. Look for the stalagmites and stalactites mentioned in the story. Cut them out along the dotted line and fold them forward along the yellow line.

Clue 2
Once you have cut out the stalagmites and stalactites and folded the sheet inward, you can see the cave behind the merging stones. Some of them have grown so far toward each other so much that there are gems wedged between them. To find the code, pay special attention to the colors of the gems and the number on the back!

Answer
From left to right, the stones have trapped a green, a red, and a yellow gem. The gems on the back of the page help you translate the colors into numbers: green has a value of 5, red has a value of 7, and yellow has a value of 3. When you enter the code 573 into the decoding strip, it will take you to page 6?

Clue 1
From page one of the book carefully cut out the square with the bat along the dotted lines, then fold it as shown on page ten. If everything is done correctly, you now have a kind of bookmark that can be placed over the corner of a book page. But when?

Clue 2
The bat symbol on page one of the book tells you where to put the bookmark over the page corners. Look for this symbol in the book (???) you will find a total of three. Once you have placed the bookmark over the page, pay special attention to the bat's teeth. They will help you find the code.

Answer
One symbol is on page 64, where the bat's teeth point to the words "first" and "eight". At the beginning of the book, you can find the symbol on page 102, where the teeth point to "three" and "six". Then on page 11 of the Secret Book, the teeth point to "last" and "3". First eight, then six, last three is the result. Enter the code 863 on the decoding strip and it will take you to page 13

Clue 1
Look at the picture on page one of the book. See the gears? They must be turned to find the correct code on page ???. You can read how many rotations you have to turn the pointers to get the correct numbers. But which way do you turn the wheels? Look at page 6 of Lucia's Secret Book for help.

Clue 2
On page ? of Lucia's Secret Book, there are three strange circles. If you really focus your eyes on one of the three circles, you will notice that the other two circles seem to be spinning. This is called an optical illusion because they are not really turning. But they show you in which direction to move the arrows to find the correct numbers.

Answer
The top pointer must be moved four positions clockwise, the middle pointer three positions counterclockwise, and the bottom pointer seven positions clockwise. The pointers will now point to the numbers ???. Enter this code on the decoding strip and you will be taken to page 52.

Clue 1
Have you taken a closer look at the legend on pages 5 and 6 of Lucas's Secret Book? Some of the words are bold and hard to hold. If you turn to page 106 of the book you'll see that there are images of these bold words. What do you think you should do with them?

Clue 2
On page 106 you will see image parts connected by a line. Find the matching words in the legend and connect them in the same way. Do you see any numbers?

Answer
When you have found and connected all 10 picture parts on page 106 of the book as shown in the legend you will see that the lines you have drawn look like numbers. They are the code you are looking for. From left to right the numbers are 1, 2, and 4. Enter 124 on the decoding strip, and it will take you to page 102.

Clue 1
On page 1 you can see a kind of maze. The other half is on page 4 of Lucas's Secret Book. Your next task is to cut out Lucas's part of the map from the book and place it next to the other half. Now you have a complete maze. And maybe pages of Lucas's Secret Book will help you even more.

Clue 2
Find the correct way through the maze. You will see an arrow pointing into the maze somewhere, this is where you start. Now all you have to do is get to the arrow pointing out at the other end. The best thing to do is to color in the space – which do amazed at what you see. Then look at the cave entrance on page 5. Can you see any connection to your maze?

Answer
Once you have colored in the maze parts of this maze will remain white running through these white areas look like a dragon, a tree, and a man. You will also have these three symbols around the coloring in the cave on pages. There you can see a 3 under the dragon, a 5 under the tree, and a 6 under the man. Reading the symbols from left to right, this gives you the code 356. Enter this on the decoding strip, and you will be taken to page 142.

Clue 1
On page 3 of Lucas's Secret Book, you will find the hexagonal stones. Cut them out and try to arrange them on the stone slab on page 18, making sure that the same symbols are always next to each other, just like in a game of dominoes. It can be quite tricky.

Clue 2
Start puzzling under the arrow with the letter A. Place one piece there so that it matches. Then find a piece that matches as the one already placed and continue with the piece next to that one. If you later had any more matching pieces, you'll know that the first one wasn't right. Remember the clue of the first place and try another one. Eventually you'll find the solution, though you may have to try all six pieces under the letter A.

Answer
Place the sixth puzzle piece under the arrow with the letter A. The rest of the pieces going clockwise are blue, orange, green, yellow, and red. The arrows marked A, B, and C point to the following symbols: dragon, sun, sun. You can use the key shown under the moon and it convert the symbols to numbers. This gives you the code 831. When you enter the code on the decoding strip, it takes you to page 95.

Clue 1
On page 7 of Lucas's Secret Book, there is a list of strange symbols. These are the cave paintings that Lucas, Anuk, and Pierce keep discovering. As the story unfolds, did you make a note of what each symbol means? Now look at the letter grid on page 135 of the book. See the symbols around the grid. What do you think you can do with them?

Clue 2
Use your map in Lucas's Secret Book to find out what each symbol means. Then find these words in the letter grid and cross them out, and only these. Can you figure out how this might help you come up with a three-digit code?

Answer
When you have crossed out all 12 words from the letter grid, you are left with a few unchecked letters. If you read these letters row by row, you will end up with the following text: THREE EIGHT FIVE exactly 385. This is the code you are looking for, and when you enter it on the decoding strip, it will take you to page 110.

DECODING MADE EASY

For each riddle, you must find a three-digit code that will take you to the page on which the story continues.

How to use the decoding strips

1. Enter the three numbers from the solved riddle by moving the colored strips on the front decoding flap so that the digits line up with the arrow.
2. Now turn the decoding flap over. The arrow will point to a new three-digit number with symbols above.
3. This three-digit code is the page number on which the story continues.
4. Check if the symbols above the digits on the decoding strips match the symbols below the page number in the book.
5. If the symbols on the book page match the symbols on your decoding strips, you have solved the riddle and can continue with the story on this page.
6. If the symbols do not match, you have not solved the riddle correctly. Please try again.

	✚	◆	⬢	●	★	☾	▲	∟	Y	■	
	0	1	0	1	0	1	0	1	0	1	

	✚	◆	⬢	●	★	☾	▲	∟	Y	■	
	9	8	7	6	5	4	3	2	1	0	

	■	Y	∟	▲	☾	★	●	⬢	◆	✚	
	9	8	7	6	5	4	3	2	1	0	

Cut out decoding strips here

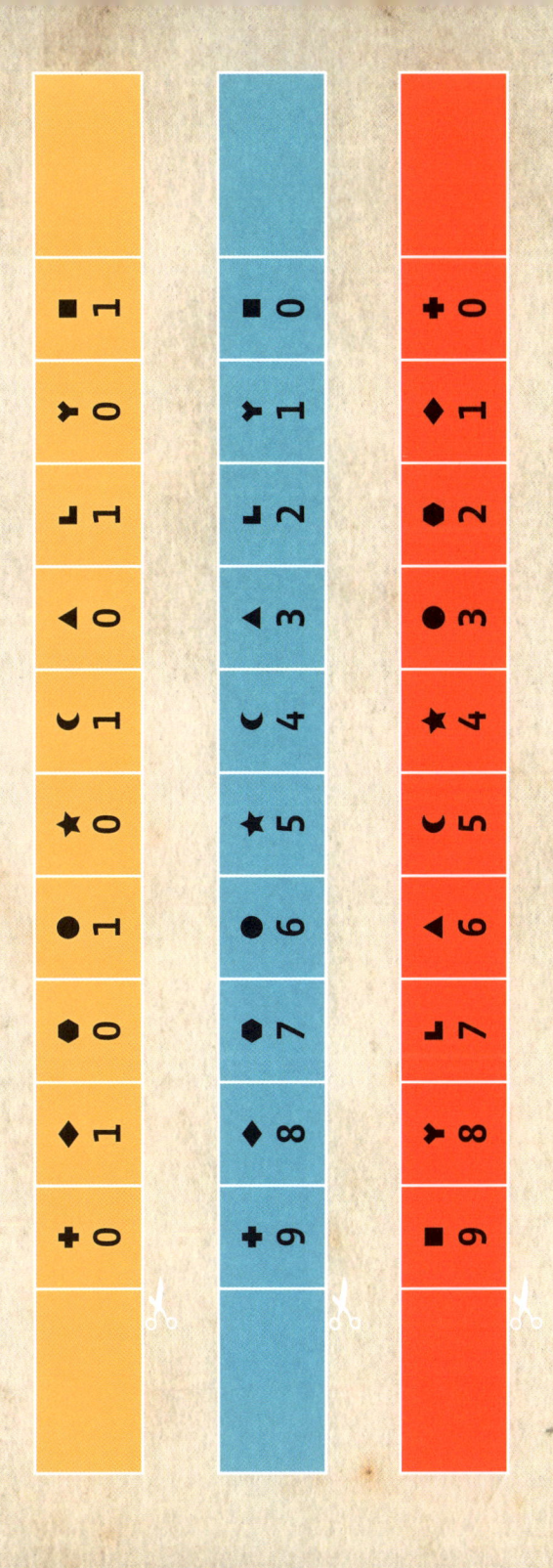

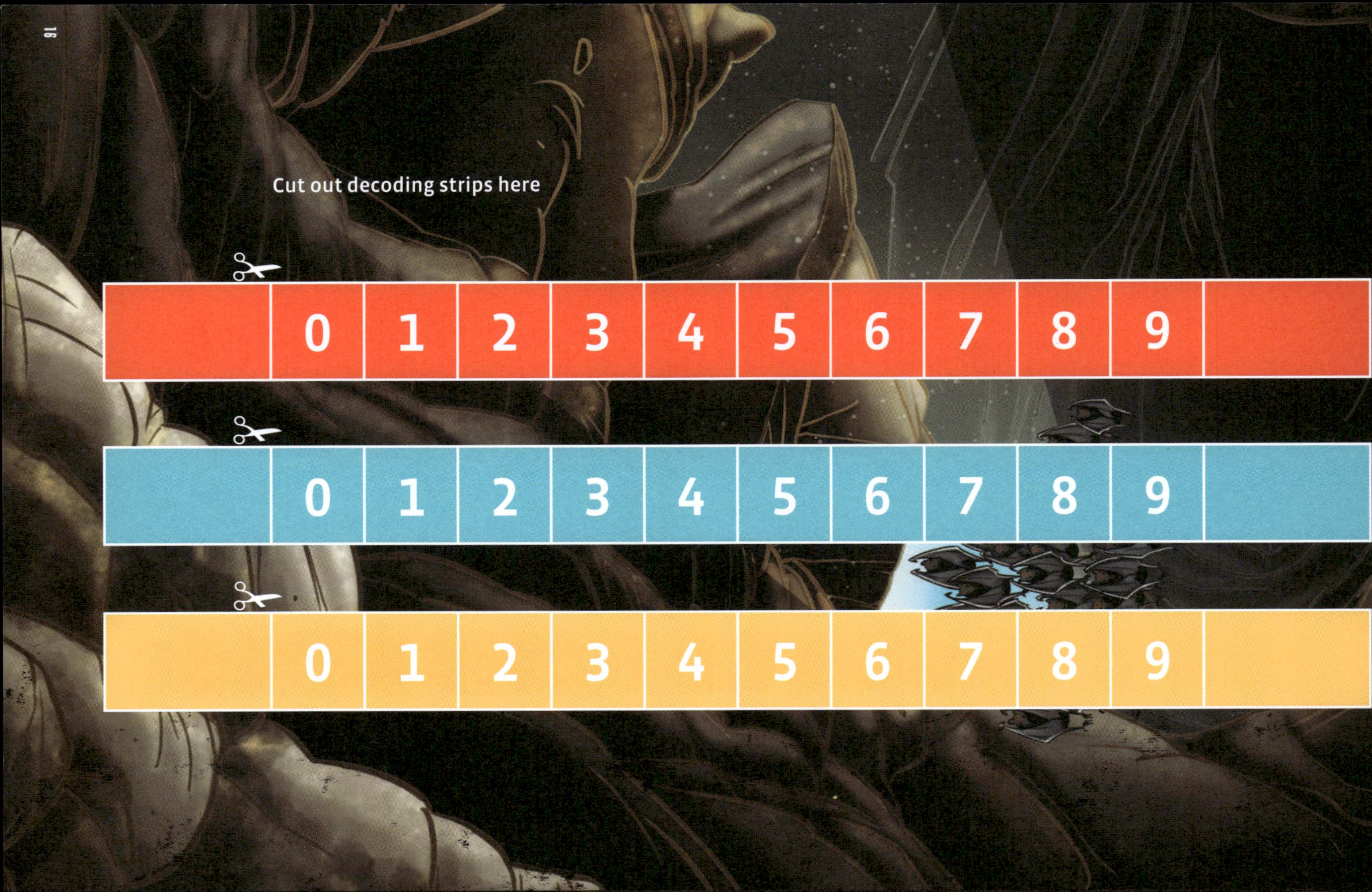

Cut out decoding strips here

	0	1	2	3	4	5	6	7	8	9	
	0	1	2	3	4	5	6	7	8	9	
	0	1	2	3	4	5	6	7	8	9	

CHALLENGE YOURSELF TO MORE PUZZLE ADVENTURES IN THE EXIT – THE BOOK SERIES!

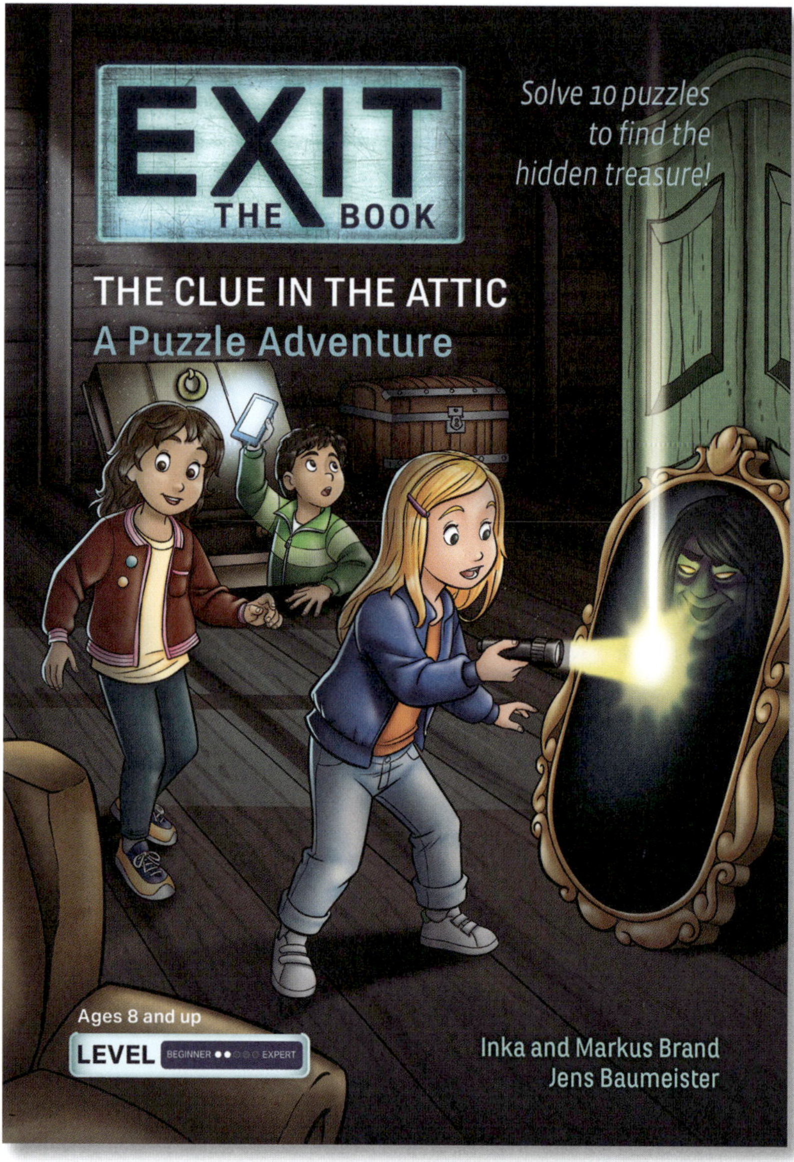
EXIT
THE BOOK
Solve 10 puzzles to find the hidden treasure!
THE CLUE IN THE ATTIC
A Puzzle Adventure
Ages 8 and up
LEVEL
BEGINNER
EXPERT
Inka and Markus Brand
Jens Baumeister

9781454958741

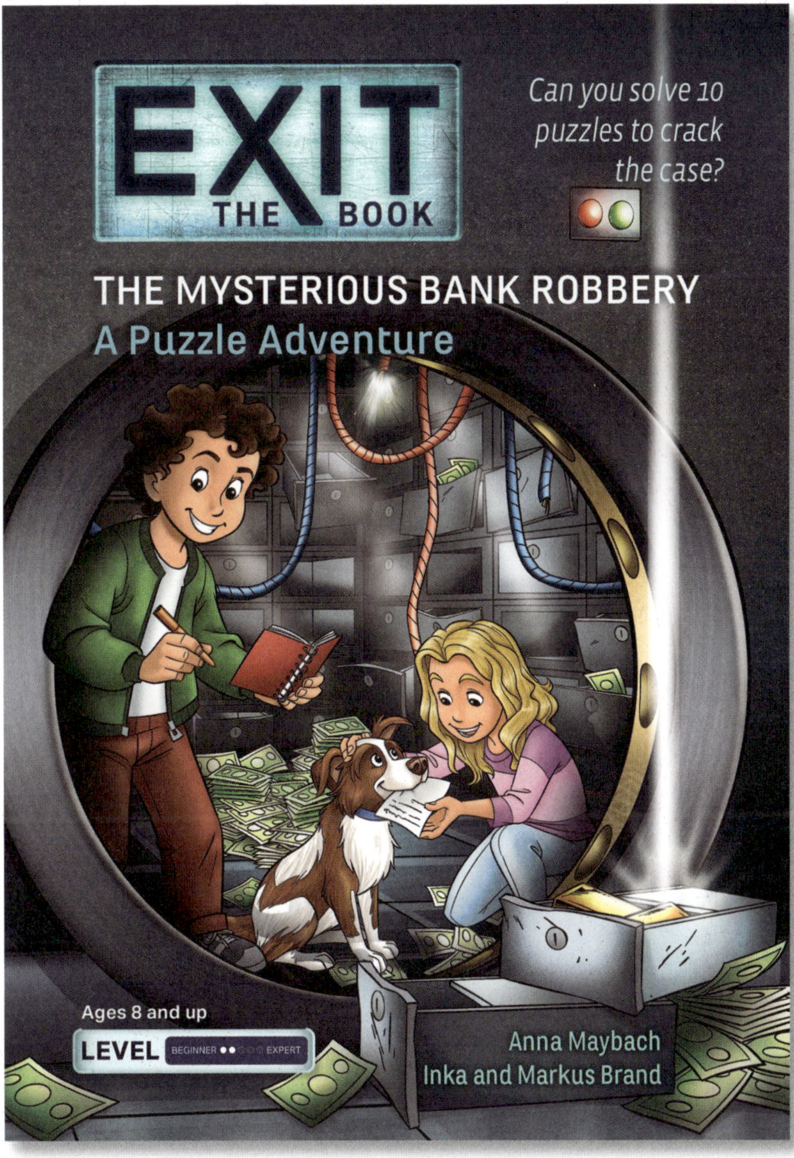
EXIT
THE BOOK
Can you solve 10 puzzles to crack the case?
THE MYSTERIOUS BANK ROBBERY
A Puzzle Adventure
Ages 8 and up
LEVEL
BEGINNER
EXPERT
Anna Maybach
Inka and Markus Brand

9781454958727

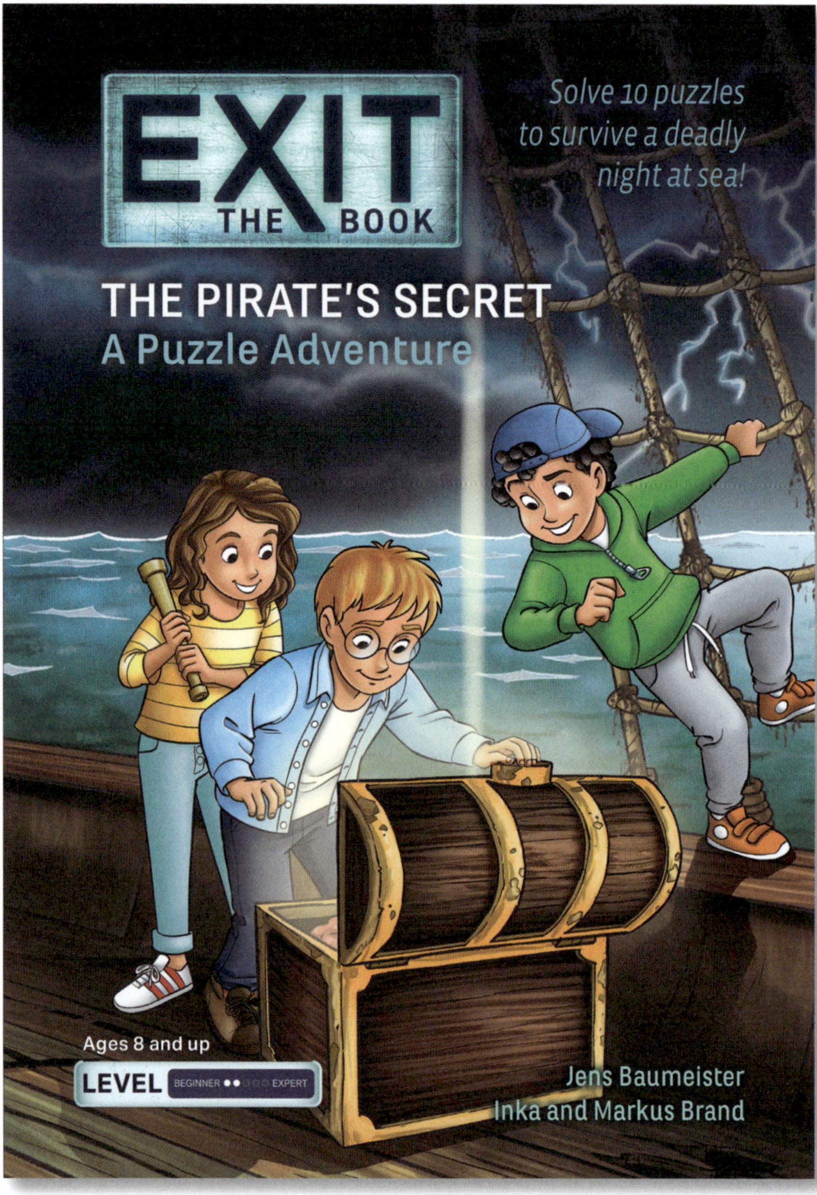
EXIT
THE BOOK
Solve 10 puzzles to survive a deadly night at sea!
THE PIRATE'S SECRET
A Puzzle Adventure
Ages 8 and up
LEVEL
BEGINNER
EXPERT
Jens Baumeister
Inka and Markus Brand

9781454958734